Praise for *W*

"When Otters Play is a fun and ac\
communities set in the beautiful Santa ~~~~~
makes the story come alive!"

– Don Barthelmess, Professor Marine Technology Department,
Santa Barbara City College

"It's no secret, I love Mara Purl's Milford-Haven, and I'm especially taken by her main character Miranda. In this story, Miranda's loneliness is more apparent than we've seen before, as she travels to events and painting excursions by herself. I can only hope that at some point she finds the ideal companion. It was heartwarming to see a small breakthrough in her relationship with her often critical mother. The big plus about reading Purl's works is what you learn, particularly about the central California coastal area, but most especially about the wildlife. You can feel the almost-human quality of the otters in this book and your heart aches for little Lulu, who is without her mother. *When Otters Play* is a wonderful read, and I was sad to reach the last page. This is another one on my 'must recommend' list."

– Linda Thompson, host of TheAuthorsShow.com

"Mara Purl once again enters the world of Milford-Haven with strong characters, interesting conflicts and a story that moves along to its final satisfying ending. *When Otters Play* deals with the plight of the otter and their relationship with humanity, but there is also a fascinating comparison Purl shows of how a mother otter relates to her young and the relationship of a human mother and her daughters. *When Otters Play* is a very well done multi-layered story that captivates readers to want to come back to Milford-Haven again and again."

– Gary Roen, syndicated reviewer and author of Journey

"Mara Purl's writing style is imaginatively eloquent. She manages to put words together in unique ways that grab my mind and make me see things I'd never thought of before. Her storytelling, simply put, is a joy. *When Otters Play* is a great read by an author who never disappoints, Mara Purl. Get it, sit down in your favorite reading chair, and enjoy."

– Roger Seiler, author of Master of Alaska

"Mara Purl creates a rich palette in her newest Milford-Haven installment. Artist Miranda Jones heads into the ocean and we meet a raft of otters as well as a mix of interesting people against a backdrop of the lush California Central Coast. All is not well at the coast, and not everyone wants to protect the otters! I love the series not only for the magical setting, but also for the author's style in bringing delicious detail to the reader. Come to Milford-Haven for the ambiance, but stay for the drama!"

– Victoria Heckman, author of the Elizabeth Murphy
Animal Communicator Series

"*When Otters Play* transports readers to the beautiful, enchanting Southern California coastal town of Milford-Haven. While Miranda Jones is developing her reputation as a serious nature artist and ascertaining her personal independence, a group of disparate characters converges, drawn by the beauty and nature of the area. Sea otters provide a backdrop for the human conflict and drama that unfolds. Find a cozy chair, pour a cup of tea, and enjoy traveling with author Mara Purl on a new adventure in the Milford-Haven series."
– Joyce B. Lohse, award-winning author of
Colorado Historical biographies

"I thoroughly enjoyed reading *When Otters Play*. As ever, your characters are vivid and very real. And, my goodness, you certainly pack a tremendous amount of information into the story. I knew nothing whatsoever about otters before reading your book. Well done!!"
– Miranda Kenrick, author of Too Far East Too Long, *Tokyo, Japan*

"A delightful tale of discovery and rescue for black-sheep (or rebel?) artist Miranda as she makes new connections with her mother and explores parallel dynamics with otter families. A new slice of life in the cast of characters of beloved Milford-Haven."
– Heidi M. Thomas, award-winning author of the Cowgirl Dreams
series and Seeking the American Dream

"Mara Purl never fails to delight me as a reader. While I love her characters (especially Miranda), I am always fully enchanted with the way she makes the marvelous landscape of California's Central Coast come alive for me. Plus, I learn something new with each story I savor: this time all the fascinating details about sea otters and their complicated, often comical, and sometimes threatened lives. I gain greater appreciation for the natural world through the eyes of this observant and authentically connected author. Kudos and applause for this newest release related to Mara's Milford-Haven series."
– Laurie Jameson

When Otters Play

Mara Purl

When Otters Play

A Milford-Haven Story

Bellekeep Books

This is a work of fiction. Names, characters, places and incidents are the product of the author's imagination or are used fictitiously, and any resemblance to actual persons, living or dead, events or locales, is entirely coincidental. The names of actual persons are used by permission.

When Otters Play © 2013 & 2017 by Mara Purl

No part of this book may be reproduced or transmitted in any form or by any means, electronic or mechanical, including photocopying, recording, or by any information storage and retrieval system, without permission in writing from the publisher. For information address: Bellekeep Books
29 Fifth Avenue, Suite 7A, New York, NY 10003
www.BellekeepBooks.com
Front Cover – Original Watercolor by Mary Helsaple ©2015
Front Cover design by Reya Patton & Kevin Meyer
©2015 by Milford-Haven Enterprises, LLC
Copy Editor: Vicki Werkley
Proofreader and Typesetter: Jean Laidig
Author photo: Lesley Bohm

Milford-Haven PUBLISHING, RECORDING & BROADCASTING HISTORY
This book is based upon the original radio drama Milford-Haven *©1987 by Mara Purl, Library of Congress numbers SR188828, SR190790, SR194010; and upon the original radio drama* Milford-Haven, U.S.A. *©1992 by Mara Purl, Library of Congress number SR232-483, broadcast by the British Broadcasting Company's BBC Radio 5 Network, and which is also currently in release in audio formats as* Milford-Haven, U.S.A. *©1992 by Mara Purl. Portions of this material may also appear on the Milford-Haven Web Site, www.MilfordHaven.com or on www.MaraPurl.com, © by Mara Purl.*
All rights reserved.

Publisher's Cataloging-In-Publication Data

Names: Purl, Mara.
Title: When otters play / Mara Purl.
Other Titles: Milford-Haven U.S.A. (Radio program) | Milford-Haven (Radio program)
Description: New York, NY : Bellekeep Books, [2017] | Series: A Milford-Haven story ;
    [bk. 3] | Based in part upon the original radio dramas Milford-Haven and Milford-
    Haven U.S.A., broadcast by BBC Radio 5 Network.
Identifiers: ISBN 9781936878833 | ISBN 9781936878635 (ebook)
Subjects: LCSH: Kayakers--California--Fiction. | Otters--California--Fiction. |
    Fishers--California--Fiction. | California--Fiction. | LCGFT: Action and adventure
    fiction.
Classification: LCC PS3566.U75 W44 2017 (print)| LCC PS3566.U75 (ebook) |
    DDC 813/.6--dc23

Published in the United States of America
E-Book Creation 2017
Bellekeep Books
ISBN (e-book): 978-1-936878-63-5
ISBN (print): 978-1-936878-83-3

Acknowledgments

Thanks: to my publishers, Tara Goff, Kara Johnson, and Patrice Samara at Belle-keep Books; to my gifted editorial team, Vicki Hessel Werkley, editor, and Jean Laidig, polish editor and layout designer; to Mary Helsaple for exquisite watercolors for my book covers; and to Kevin Meyer and Modern Alchemy for superb cover design and graphics.

Thanks to Jonatha King for PR and marketing; Amber Ludwig and Sky Esser for Internet design and wizardry; and Kelly Johnson for Social Media expertise and creativity.

Thanks to those who provided expertise during my research. On wildlife painting—artists Mary Helsaple and Caren Pearson. On sea otters—Erin Lenihan with the sea otter program at Monterey Bay Aquarium; and Brian Hatfield with the U.S. Geological Survey, who monitors and cares for sea otters in the wild along the Central Coast of California. On commercial fishing and commercial diving—Don Barthelmess, Professor of Marine Technology Training at Santa Barbara City College; and Doug Herzick, commercial fisherman.

To the best of my ability, I've represented all scientific data accurately. Two events I include in the story did actually happen, but are somewhat fictionalized. The first is the San Diego Zoo Gala, a real event, but fictionalized here to include Roger Payne visiting with my character Miranda. I did have the honor of sitting next to the extraordinary Dr. Payne at a gala, but it was in 1993 in San Pedro, rather than in 1997 in San Diego, as the story portrays. The other is the mass exodus of the sea otters, which did happen, but in 1998, one year later than the setting of my story.

And most important of all—thanks to *you*, my readers! I'm thrilled to welcome those of you who are new to my books. And I extend a special heartfelt thanks to the core group of readers who've been with me from the beginning and are continuing with me on the journey.

Dear Reader —

Welcome to Milford-Haven! If this is your inaugural visit, it's my pleasure to introduce you to my favorite little town and to a few of its many residents—all of whom are described in the Cast of Characters for the series near the end of the book.

This novella features artist Miranda Jones, and gives you a glimpse of her life as a wildlife artist. The story stands alone as a complete tale, but also is woven into the overall tapestry of the Milford-Haven saga. Chronologically, *When Otters Play* occurs just before *Why Hearts Keep Secrets*, book three of the Milford-Haven Novels. Indeed, to give you a seamless transition—and to let you pick up the first thread of the ongoing mystery—you'll find the Prologue and Chapter One of the third novel are waiting for you after the short story.

In this story we travel with Miranda to Santa Barbara, a town of opulence and benevolence, political strife and environmental awareness. It takes you into the unique coastal waters where sea otters live. And it takes you to the mysterious and magical Channel Islands. The story is set in 1997 and some of the political and ecological issues described have been resolved, though maintaining the delicate balance is forever a challenge.

This brief sojourn to California's only south-facing coastline—America's Riviera—is part history, part imagination, and part the pure joy of peering into the lives of those who live on and under our coastal waters.

As this short e-book unfolds, follow the wake of my boat through the interconnected pathways of those who inhabit Milford-Haven, and come to that timeless place where otters can play.

Mara Purl

"Play so that you may be serious."
– Anarchis

"There's mind in the waters. And that's not all.
There's heart in the waters, too."
– Miranda Jones

When Otters Play

1

Miranda Jones!"

Miranda slammed the trunk of her Mustang.

"Do something with that hair!"

Miranda's mother stepped closer and reached up to comb fingers through her daughter's long, flyaway strands. "The new cut is marvelous, but you still have to *style* it, dear. Would you like to take my hair spray with you?"

"No, Mom. But thanks. Time for me to hit the road."

"Drive carefully." She gave her child a fierce hug. "There are crazy people on the road these days. Call me when you get to your apartment."

"I will."

"And call me when you get to Santa Barbara tomorrow."

"Right. Love you." Miranda pulled herself away, the urge to flee fighting with the guilt of leaving. She climbed into her Mustang, slammed the door and started the motor.

"Don't forget to give my best to Zelda!" her mother called.

But I won't be seeing her, Miranda wanted to shout back, though she'd already explained this. It was exhausting, trying to synch her mother's rhythms with her own. She wanted to gun the engine and spit gravel as she tore down the driveway. Instead, she summoned the energy to turn around and wave.

Veronica "Very" Jones still stood in the front doorway. *If I don't wave, I'll be eaten up with guilt all the way back to Milford-Haven.* Stifling a moan, and forcing a smile, Miranda dutifully lifted an arm to make the family-signature gesture: an oversized infinity sign drawn through the air.

As she did, time seemed to suspend for a moment, and she glimpsed her parent, not as the bullying authority she so often presented, but as a hauntingly vulnerable woman who'd ventured her *all* into the safe-keeping of her husband and daughters. Then, like a wisp of cloud, the image vanished, replaced by the proverbial steel magnolia standing in the imposing front entrance to the Jones family mansion.

Two nights earlier, at the start of the first weekend in February, Miranda had arrived home for a visit. Not "home," she corrected herself. She'd moved out long ago, and her own home was now in Milford-Haven, the tiny town just south of San Simeon on the spectacular and sparsely populated stretch of the California coastline.

But not *once* through a long evening of dinner in the dining room, followed by coffee in the living room, had either of her parents actually acknowledged that she now lived in the small town she'd chosen. They referred to her living there as a phase, a lark, or an experiment. "You know, Miranda," her father had intoned, "if you insist on postponing your adult career, why don't you at least get another degree out of it? Look how well Meredith is doing with her MBA."

There was never any point in defending herself against her father's criticisms, implied or otherwise. And there was no mileage in arguing. Miranda had cleared her dishes and bidden her parents good night. As she'd walked through the corridor into the kitchen, she'd overheard her mother say, "Oh, Charles," in that familiar reprimand.

"What? What did I say?" As she started up the stairs, Miranda imagined her father's hands thrown up in frustration. She made a point not to listen to any more of their conversation.

The next morning, Miranda awoke in the home where she'd enjoyed a privileged childhood as the younger of two beautiful, precocious brunette daughters.

The traditional Tudor now seemed an embarrassing display of excess that would've looked more suitable a century earlier as a country estate somewhere outside of London. This was her own bias, she realized, from her current perspective as an environmentalist and liberal.

During her childhood, the family home had seemed nothing short of magical, a place where she and her sister had imagined themselves as every sort of princess, from historic to galactic, complete with costumes and castles. Secluded in three acres of gardens, gazebos and forest, the home rose three stories from a sprawling foundation, holding a vast kitchen, two dining rooms, twelve bedrooms, and . . . she'd lost count of how many bathrooms. Though as a child, she'd found the home a delight as her vivid imagination transformed it to an orbiting space station or a remote Castle—dungeons and parapets, inclusive—now she couldn't imagine how two adults could justify living in such an oversized monolith.

I have to admit, Mother does use every single room. It was true. Board meetings for the Ballet were held in the second dining room, whose walls were constantly festooned with the current season's posters and autographed glossies of the premiere dancers.

Miranda shook her head against the pillow in the cozy double bed, which now seemed small compared to the king-sized mattress she enjoyed at home. But mother had done some updates to this sweet room that'd been her childhood sanctuary. The cheerful yellow-checked curtains, coverlet, and shams she'd been so thrilled about at age twelve—her sister's room had been done in pinks and fuchsias—had been replaced. Now the room had been redone in soothing shades of green: moss walls, celadon duvet, bright peridot silk throw pillows. Two chests of drawers framed a narrow window seat—its cushions covered in sturdy twill. *She chose my favorite colors*, Miranda realized with a twinge of remorse. *I didn't think she cared, or even noticed. But this room is lovely. Perfect, actually.*

Rolling out of bed, Miranda raised the sage-colored blind and peered out the mullioned window into the back garden. The forsythia of early spring formed a curving border in this section of the grounds, brightening the foggy dawn more than sunshine could. *Beautiful. Inspired. I should paint it one day.*

She paused to listen for a moment. No birdsong outside; no stirrings inside. *This would be a perfect time to take myself on a tour of the second floor, before anyone notices.* Pulling her chenille robe over the silk pajamas she'd brought to wear at her parents' home, Miranda opened her bedroom door and closed it quietly behind her, then began to tiptoe down the hall.

Next to hers, her sister's bedroom had also been redone, Miranda now saw. The walls were covered in a muted teal raw silk wallpaper, and the room had a more finished look than her own. *Paintings on the walls, china from mother's collection placed on the bookshelf and chests.* Their mother had made a study of the china and porcelain of Asia and Europe, and had passed some of her knowledge to her girls. On the heavy, antique furniture rested blue-and-white Imari china, paired here and there with the Delftware counterpoints that had appeared in the mid-seventeenth century when Dutch artisans began to copy the original Oriental designs. The duvet and Regency chair were covered in watered taffeta, with velvet and lime colored throw pillows added in a medley of blues. *It's a blue symphony. Mer must absolutely love it! I know she gets home a lot more often than I do.*

"Home." There was that word again. Would this edifice, with all its memories, always be as impossible to escape as it seemed at this moment? How would she and her sister feel after her parents . . . if they ever sold, or . . . when they passed on? Miranda shuddered at the thought, and stepped back into the corridor.

A few yards farther along, the door to her father's stamp room stood open. As it was the room nearest the master suite, she took care not to make a sound as she entered, hoping a squeaky floorboard wouldn't give her away. Even now, she hardly dared enter this "sacred space" her dad had carved out to pursue his favorite hobby.

He'd put the room to good use. Framed copies of rare

stamps decorated the walls, along with his certificates of achievement. Her gaze took in the detail of his orderly desk. Like old-fashioned wooden fonts stored in printer's drawers, philatelic paraphernalia sat in carefully arranged, segmented trays: glassine envelopes and stamp hinges, tongs and water-marking fluid, a perf gauge and showguard mounts, and a mini stamp guillotine. This kind of space she understood. This was *artist* space, a place to work with the correct tools handily within reach, a place to focus and drink in the detail of the work, each stamp a tiny painting as fully realized as a huge canvas.

If only Dad realized this is something we have in common, the love of detail and accuracy, the choice of color and propor-tion, the understanding of perspective, the capturing of a mo-ment where wildlife and humans cross paths.

Her father collected all kinds of stamps, and was pressing toward the mark of being one of the only collectors ever to amass one copy of each American stamp. But as extraordinary a landmark as this would be, she'd always known his favorites were those in his Duck Stamp Collection. Wildlife artists com-peted annually for the coveted prize. *I've entered several times, but never won. Winning it would probably be the only way I'd ever earn his respect. Good luck with that.*

The walls of his collection room were carefully hung with framed works, some of them the originals that later became stamps. *But as many of my own pieces as I've sent to him—some of them even framed—none are hung in here. Maybe when I paint the otters, he'll like that. But I doubt it.*

She reached out to pick up the one framed photograph on the desk: a family portrait taken years earlier. *Here we all are, starched and ironed, backs straight and eyes forward. If the image were sepia-toned, I could believe it was taken a hundred years earlier.*

Her father: strict and demanding one minute, he could sometimes be a marshmallow the next. Beauty and feminine wiles almost always charmed him, and she'd seen any number of times when Mother or Mer went to work on him. But in Miranda's opinion, she herself possessed almost none of these. When it came to intellectual rigor, his world-view didn't allow that an artist had any—unless he committed himself to realism and research. Wildlife artists who won competitions were disqualified if they painted an animal outside its native habitat, so *they* passed muster in his book. But they were exceptions to the rule.

Most true discipline and success came only to those who labored in the fields of business, with a few academic exceptions to that rule. As such, Miranda's sister Meredith fulfilled their dad's idea of proper work and proper pay. Mer had it made with their paternal parental unit, except, of course, that she hadn't been born a boy. Yet her gifted sister had virtually surmounted even that obstacle. *At what cost, though? Is Mer really doing what she loves? Or what she thinks she must in order to bask in that golden parental glow?*

Miranda heard a stirring beyond the door that led to her parents' master suite. Frozen in place for a moment, when she heard her father's voice, she spun and dashed out into the corridor, then tiptoed down the stairs, her toes sinking into the plush carpet that lined the center of each step. When she reached the kitchen, she flipped on the lights, found an Earl Gray tea bag, placed it in a mug, then filled it by pressing the slender hot-water lever installed along the back rim of the kitchen sink. While fragrant steam rose from the steeping brew, Miranda carried it to the garden room. Ana would be here soon to make breakfast, and her parents would come down sometime during the next hour. Till then, she could wrap herself in a throw, sip her tea, and look out at the foggy garden.

I shouldn't be so hard on them, she thought, as she settled in a wide floral-cushioned window seat. *They love us. They mean well. They want the best for us.* Dad definitely had his good points. And in any case, pinning her hopes on changing his mind about her career would be like trying to make a lighthouse change course. He was fixed in one place, and always would be. There was a certainty in him that provided stability for the family.

As her thoughts returned to her mother, the irritation began to surface again. Mother—obviously as artistic as her younger daughter—nevertheless refused to admit that creativity had any use other than as a distraction, a pleasant hobby, or a domestic responsibility. Women weren't supposed to have *real* careers. They were supposed to get a decent education, then turn their attentions to marriage and family. "Otherwise, Miranda, how will society ever flourish, or even continue? If there's no one to support the schools and the churches, the museums and the ballets, what will become of them?"

"But, Mother," Miranda had argued, "if there are no dancers to dance, and no painters to paint, your point is moot."

"I will not be muted, Miranda," her mother had countered, misunderstanding the word.

Very Jones was a self-made woman, though this was not the impression she wished to make. In her generation, "self-made" was only a flattering epithet for men, certainly not for women, who were supposed to have been carefully groomed and prepared since childhood to take their places in the bedroom and the non-profit boardroom. Very, born in a small West Virginia town, had graduated from high school and married the man of her dreams—and those of her parents—before embarking on a brilliant domestic career. But the fact that she'd never attended college was sometimes so humiliating to her that she'd either bluster her way into an argument, or withdraw in a pout worthy of the French nobility—behavior she justified by reminding her husband or any family members who happened to be nearby that she came by honestly, as the descendant of a Gaulish noble. To avoid the pout, Miranda refrained from explaining the difference between "moot" and "mute."

"I am heard very clearly in the boardroom, I can assure you," her mother continued. "Of course we need dancers! But these people are *born* to dance, and they have absolutely nothing else in their lives. Think how few of them make it into a decent dance company! And think how short a time they have in which to dance at this level! We must support them, or the entire art will vanish."

They'd had it before, this same argument, and what Miranda found so frustrating was that she and her mother had at least as many points of agreement as they did divergent views. It's just that Mother's world-view was composed of a series of boxes, and though one of these was labeled "artists," her very own daughter was and always would be ineligible for that category. Instead, Miranda was to be placed—kicking and screaming if necessary—into the box labeled "wife and mother."

Not that I never want to marry or have a family. But not now, not before I've made something of my work, established my own sense of . . . what? Identity? Purpose? She took a sip from the mug of tea, then wrapped her fingers around it to warm them. *They have it all planned for me, and if I vary from their map, I'm doing something wrong. Maybe that's why I'm glad Zack Calvin hasn't called. He's almost too perfect. He'd fit into this family better than I do!*

"Miranda?"

She heard her mother calling from the foot of the stairs.

"In here, Mother!"

"Come join me in the kitchen!"

The carefully scheduled day with her parent was about to begin.

2

The California Coastal sea otter rolled herself out of the last, long branch of kelp in which she'd wrapped herself for sleep. On her nose, she bore a distinctive white sickle-shaped tattoo—a mating scar that'd now mostly healed.

She clutched the satiny pelt of her pup to ensure he didn't slide off her belly and slip under the waves. Now she untangled his body from the extra kelp strands she used these days to prevent their combined weight from carrying them away in the tide.

For another moment she and her offspring floated in the silken gray waves under a barely lightening sky while she tuned her ears for the mournful sound of the pup she'd lost so long ago. She still heard him sometimes, his high-pitched wails strafing across the Santa Barbara coastal waters to pierce her heart. Time and again, she'd tried without success to lumber her way across the barriers that divided them.

Now, her mother-heart was filled with the joys and duties that'd arrived with her new delivery. Warm and vulnerable, his baby-heart beat against hers in the waters of the bay. Raising her head, she used her vibrissa—highly sensitized whiskers—to feel unusual vibrations in the water, then listened for any sound of danger. Sensing none, she stretched and yawned, blinking to activate her cat-like night vision.

The urgent squeals of her pup reminded her what her priorities were.

Hungry. Must eat.

3

Dave Dax sipped from the oversized mug bearing his company's logo—D&D Channel Charters—and winced as the scalding coffee etched its way across his tongue and down his gullet. "Geez, that's hot!" he complained to his computer as it continued to boot. "But it gets the juices flowing."

Before opening the office this morning, Dave had made his customary check of the three boats they owned—shining in the lemon-yellow light, tethered in their slips and pulling gently at their lines, as if eager to escape the marina. He glanced at his watch, glad he'd come in even earlier than usual this morning, avoiding the increasingly annoying Santa Barbara rush hour, to keep a phone date with their new bookkeeper. Before he was trapped at this desk, he was eager to get the printer warming up, set out the brochure racks, and unbolt the equipment locker his partner Doug would need later this morning.

Right on time, the phone rang precisely as the wall clock struck 8 a.m.

"D&D Charters," he answered, grabbing the handset on the first ring.

"Good morning, Dave. This is Sandra Sandowski. Ready to answer a few questions?"

"Well, you sound chipper this a.m., like you've already been up for hours."

"Oh, I have," she agreed, her voice bright and almost as electric as the wires over which it traveled. "I never miss a sunrise. Best time of the day."

"Ditto. Only time I get enough quiet to think, and enough space to run."

"You're a runner?"

"Oh, yeah. You?"

"I love running."

He decided to test to see what she actually meant by that. *A pansy who likes the outfits more than the sport?* "Avocado?" he asked.

"Last October on the Carpenteria Bluffs? That was so much fun."

"So you do 5Ks."

"Some of them," she confirmed. "I mean, that was the twentieth annual. Couldn't miss that one."

"Right," Dave said, impressed.

"I'm signed up for the Orchard to Ocean next month, too," she enthused.

"The 10K . . . yeah, so am I."

"And it's their fifth annual," she added.

Just how good a runner is this woman? Maybe she's a whole lot better than I am! "I, uh, don't suppose you're signed up for the Pier to Peak, are you?"

A bright laugh trilled over the phone line. "Not likely! Four thousand foot elevation? That's one of the hardest runs in the state!"

Somewhat relieved . . . or reassured—he wasn't sure which—Dave responded with a laugh of his own, though he sounded like a nervous heron. "Right. I wanna do it one of these years, though."

"Then you must be a *great* runner!"

Dave laughed again, this time sounding to his own ears like a harbor seal. "I don't know about that!"

"I suppose we oughtta get some work done," she suggested.

"Right! Yes! Okay. What do you need?"

"Well, I can't quite work out the different aspects of your business, so if you wouldn't mind giving me an overview, that'd be a good place to start."

"Yeah, absolutely. So, one part of it—my part, mostly—is the harbor and coastline charter business. We offer kayak tours. And then we also do day-tours where my partner Doug takes them on motorized skiffs out to the islands."

"The Channel Islands?" she asked.

"Right. And it takes a couple of hours to get out there, whether it's to Anacapa, or Santa Cruz Island. Those are all-day tours. They run $150."

"Got it. So let's talk about the harbor first. Seems kind of busy to be allowing small boats to wander around."

"True. We actually let people rent kayaks, and show them where things will be most interesting, either by giving them a guided tour, or by giving them a chart and a time limit by which they have to get the kayaks back to us."

He heard Sandra sigh over the phone. "Sounds like such a blast. Just curious, where exactly do you take people on the guided tours?"

"Uh, when we head out, we take them to the Sand Spit, then we might circle some of the buoys if the sea-lions are sunbathing."

Sandra chuckled.

"Then, you know, we just paddle from the Wharf all the way along the waterfront."

"Do you give newbies a paddling lesson?"

"Oh, yeah. That's critical. It's not just the paddling, it's training in how to deal with the kayak if it flips, how to get out from under it, how to aim it if you get into some waves, you know, a bunch of things."

"Which sounds like you eventually go beyond the harbor."

"We do, yeah. We take people past some pretty secluded beaches, we skim over at least one kelp forest where there's a lot of marine life—otters and sea lions and lots of fish species. I might talk about local history, marine ecology—"

"Oh, so *you're* the tour guide?"

"Right, it's usually me, though during our busy summer season, we take on some local hires who know their stuff."

"Okay, this business unit includes equipment rental, professional tour guiding, safety training. . . . "

Dave heard her keyboard clacking through the phone, then glanced at his watch, noting he still had a half hour before he had to open the shop.

"Anything else?" she asked.

"Uh, well, we order catering for these tours. We stop at one of the beaches about halfway through the tour, pull the kayaks ashore and spread out some mats. The brown-bag lunches are really good. We buy 'em from Sand Castles Café."

"Are these lunches gull-proof?"

Dave paused for a moment before realizing she'd made

a joke. "What? No, sadly, no. Far as I know, *nothing* edible is gull-proof."

Chuckling again, Sandra continued, "Okay so add 'catering' to the list of goods and services offered. Got it."

"Yeah, and then we just do a big loop and paddle back into the harbor. Makes for a nice day."

"Sounds perfect to me. And do people bring their own gear?"

"Uh, well, some people do, but for most customers we have paddle jackets, helmets and even wetsuits if it's really chilly."

"Aha, so I need to add equipment rental to the list of services. What about snorkeling?"

"Not on these harbor kayak trips. That comes under the second part of the business."

"Oh, okay, so for now, talking about the harbor-part, these are what, four-hour trips?"

"Right."

"And the rate?"

"It's thirty bucks just to rent the kayak, or it's fifty if you want the guided tour."

"Got it. And you said it's seasonal, right?"

"Well, we do get business all year. I mean, the weather in Santa Barbara is fantastic like, what, ninety percent of the time? But then things pick up when kids are out of school and families from other parts of the country come into town. Spring break, too, can get busy."

Dave listened to her typing for another moment, then offered, "Say, you wouldn't want to come on a tour with me, would you? No charge. We'll call it a business expense, so you can understand what we do better."

There was a moment of silence before Sandra replied, "I was *really* hoping you'd say that! Yes, I'd love to come."

"Great. Like, next week?"

"Uh, I think so. For now, I should really get these categories all set up in QuickBooks, see about your first quarter sales for tax filing, all that stuff."

"Ugh. Better you than I. We do really appreciate your taking this over for us."

"Happy to have your business! Okay, so wanna tell me about Doug's side of your partnership? Oh, and is it a partnership, or an LLC?"

"Partnership."

"Okay, good. So Doug takes people out on your skiff. You own one boat?"

"Three, actually. And Doug does other stuff, too."

"Other stuff?"

"Yeah, he should tell you more of the details, and I know he wants your help doing all his other bookkeeping too."

"He has other partnerships?"

"No, no, he does three things. He's a commercial diver. You know, the guys that go down to the ocean floor with umbilical cords?"

"Uh, I've heard of them."

"Yeah, unbelievable. Anyway, he works on offshore oil rigs. And then during his off season, he dives to supply local restaurants. Between those two jobs, he takes our clients out on diving trips and boat tours."

"Wow, that's quite the schedule!" Sandra observed.

"He's a hard worker. Everyone who works the waterfront is, one way or another." Dave glanced at his clock, wondering how much longer the call would take. Customers could be showing up any time, now, and he had a few more things to do before opening the doors. He liked talking with Sandra, though, and had the feeling this new bookkeeper would work out just fine.

4

As the new family chauffeur opened the door to the Lincoln Town Car, Miranda smiled, feeling embarrassed at the special treatment she no longer experienced on a regular basis. Ueno-san—the beloved employee who'd driven the Jones girls to school through most of their childhood—had long since retired and now lived in the beautiful retirement home her parents had arranged for him, and still paid for. The new man seemed to be Eastern European and had an old-world elegance about him. *Mother thinks he's the best thing since sliced brioche.*

Her mother arrived, now, bustling out of the house, down the front steps and into the right rear passenger seat, so that she could easily see and speak with her driver. "We're off to Gump's, Mr. Milovich," she said brightly. "A day of shopping with my daughter!"

Miranda, startled by the absolute joy in her mother's voice, turned to look at her parent, who now beamed back at her. "Won't this be fun?" she asked, though it was more a declaration than a question.

Miranda couldn't help but smile back. "It will," she said, wondering if, for once, perhaps it might be. The prospect of shopping with Mom had always held more dread than enjoyment, for where Miranda found it exhausting, Very always seemed to gather more energy even as she collected treasures in one department or store after another. Un-fond memories of being dragged in and out of dressing rooms played in her mind like vintage home movies. But, as the car began its journey on the narrow, winding road that led down from their perch atop Belvedere Island, a mental slide show flashed images of her child-self twirling in adorable little-girl dresses.

"Spring is just about to bloom, and both of us need new dresses for the season," her mother began. "I know you favor solid colors, and for that matter, so do I, normally. But I've seen some bold floral prints in my magazines, and some of them are brilliantly flattering."

"I have no place to wear a floral dress, Mother." Miranda heard the bitter complaint in her own voice. "I mean, it's unlikely," she amended, trying for less harshness in her tone.

"You do have your special art events. In any case, that's the thing about spring. You never know what lovely thing might happen."

To that, Miranda couldn't think of a single objection. Nor could she remember when her mother had sounded so positive.

"Shall we say two hours, Mr. Milovich?" Very asked, when the driver pulled smoothly to the front door of Gump's.

"Yes, Madame. And you may reach me on the car phone, should your plans change."

"Very good. And then we'll go somewhere for luncheon."

Moments later, the two women were inside, inhaling the cool, spicy home-fragrance that wafted through the store's polished corridors and across its counters. Miranda heard her mother murmur "Divine" under her breath, and smiled at her obvious pleasure.

Suddenly making a sharp turn to the right, Very stared at a sign. "Oriental Design," she proclaimed, marching off toward said objects. "The lines can be very simple, you know. Polished wood, dark hardware. Might suit your décor quite well."

A day of surprises, thought Miranda. "You . . . how do you know about my décor?"

"How would I *not* know, dear. No harm in looking."

The next thing she knew, Miranda stood face to face with one of the most beautiful cabinets she'd ever seen. Just as her mother'd said, it was made of some dark, polished wood, with shelves, cubbies, and cabinets fitted with iron pulls and hinges. A wall unit with modules that seemed interchangeable, it was structured with each column of squares higher than the next giving it a stair-step profile.

"Don't you have stairs?" her mother asked.

"Yes. They lead down from my living room to my bedroom."

"Right. An upside-down house. Well, a set of descending stairs could be set off by this piece. Ascending would be better, of course, but we work with what we have."

Mom is right. If I can ever buy my building . . . and if I ever have the budget to add a third story . . . a set of stairs climbing upward from my living room would offer a loft with an unobstructed ocean view. . . . "Uh, right. So this piece would sit on the bottom floor alongside the stairs. The top of it would be visible—"

"—from the living room," Very interrupted. "Exactly. And with some of your pots placed, it could look quite interesting."

"My pots? Right. They would," Miranda replied, once again stunned at her mother's awareness of her taste and of her pottery pieces.

"Let's get the price. No point in dreaming without knowing what we're looking at."

Price? She thinks I can even begin to afford something like this? Maybe I should be flattered.

"Well, the damage isn't all that terrible," her mother reported. "The tag says $1100.00. Shall we put it on your credit card, or mine?"

"But Mother," Miranda began, "I don't—"

"Don't say you don't love it, because I saw in your eyes that you fell in love at first sight. And as for can't? Who says? You're selling your work. You can pay me back."

And before Miranda could stop her, Very was off to find the cashier while her daughter stood there too shocked to object. *She's a freight train. I don't think I could stop her if I tried. And . . . I can always return it, I suppose, or just call and cancel the order. That might work better than rushing over there to tell the clerk I changed my mind. That would only hurt Mom's feelings.*

On the one hand, Miranda felt resigned, as she so often did in the face of her mother's force of will. On the other hand, some small part of her felt a thrill at the prospect of having something of beauty and value that actually did perfectly match her own taste. *Not a French antique. Not an expensive lamp with a frilly white shade. Not a bright red Chinese lacquer table. Not anything my sister would choose for her own home. But something I'll really use and love.*

"Done," her mother pronounced. "They'll deliver it in two weeks, so just make sure you're home."

"I . . . You . . . Thank you, Mom." Miranda kissed her mother's cheek.

"Now, now, you're going to pay me back for it, dear, just remember that. And we won't mention this to your father, for now. This will be a little arrangement between you and me. You can send me a check for $100 the first of every month. Agreed?"

"Okay."

"Now. Time to look at clothes."

Tempted to groan as she would have at age twelve, this time Miranda nodded, and followed the footsteps on her mother's very elegant but low-heeled Christian Louboutin pumps as they clacked on the marble floor.

Her mother spun to look back at her. "Don't you have an event coming up?"

Miranda blinked. "An event?"

"You mentioned something over the holidays, but at the time we were all too busy to do anything about it. A party. They're showing your work."

"Oh, right, the San Diego Zoo."

"Well, I suppose even zoos have fancy parties, don't they? For their fund-raising?"

"Actually, they do. This will be their annual gala. On February fourteenth."

"Valentine's Evening! And they're introducing you as the artist who did their latest commission! Well, we *must* find you something purrrrr-fect, mustn't we?"

Miranda couldn't help but smile at her mother's enthusiasm. *She'll use any excuse to shop for a gown. Now . . . to keep her from choosing something with ruffles.*

By thirty minutes later, Very had chosen several dresses. She'd insisted Miranda sit in the dressing room and wait to see her selections. She and the saleswoman helping her bustled in, holding hangers high enough to keep the long skirts from dragging on the floor. "Now, before you say anything, Miranda dear, just promise me you'll *try* them all. Things look different on hangers than they do on the body."

"Yes, Mother."

"Good girl."

Wouldn't you know, the first dress has ruffled sleeves! Miranda bit her tongue, and let the royal blue chiffon confection drift over her up-stretched arms. The three women— Miranda, Very, and the clerk—all stared at the reflection in the three-way mirror.

"No, I don't think so," Very said decisively.

With relief, Miranda removed the garment. A moment later, they stared together at the next offering: burgundy silk, simple bodice, full skirt.

"Lovely for the holidays. Not right for the Zoo," Very pronounced.

At this comment, the sales clerk looked confused.

"She's to be honored by the San Diego Zoo. She's a very well-known artist, you know."

The clerk nodded and smiled politely while Miranda rolled her eyes. Very pulled a red dress off its hanger.

"Oh, Mother, really?"

"I know, I know, you always say you don't like red. But it likes *you* because of your coloring. And it is for Valentine's."

Submitting once again, Miranda allowed the slinky fabric to skim down and hug her slender curves.

"Oh," Miranda said.

"My," the sales clerk remarked.

"That's the one," Very said. "Simple. Elegant. And it's that fabric you like, the one you call 'indestructible.' Probably a good idea, considering where you'll be wearing it."

Another hour later, Miranda winced as her heels met the smoothly tiled floor. *Only a hundred steps to go before we make it to the escalator.* Her hand smarted where the string-handles of the heavy shopping bag bit into her fingers, and the small of her back was beginning to ache.

But one look at the figure of her mother leading on to greater shopping glories, and Miranda knew she'd have to find her second—or third—wind. Very Jones's step was still light, her eagerness to find the next treasure still keen.

I think I understand it better now. It's the visions she has in her head that drives her, not the searching. Looking for something with a sense of purpose and expectation . . . that's something I do understand. I just don't usually find that kind of pleasure in looking for material objects. But she did find me the perfect dress for the gala. I should do something nice for her, now.

"Mother," she called. "I have an idea."

Very turned. "Yes?"

"May I treat you to tea at the Rotunda?"

"Oh, at Neiman's?"

"We could sit under that gorgeous Beaux-arts glass dome. It's only a couple of blocks."

"Well, that's a lovely idea, Miranda. I accept!" She began to fish in her purse. "Now, I'll have to call Mr. Milovich on that mobile phone your father insisted I carry."

Miranda smiled. *Mother adores Neiman Marcus. I'll just have to steer her directly to the fourth floor tea room so she doesn't have a chance to shop for more clothes!*

5

Sunlight shot its first beams across the manicured trees
and angled roofs of Santa Barbara. Lancing over the
4,000-foot mountains that squeezed the town against
the coastline, the brightness gleamed on the waters of the
Channel that lapped the shoreline and floated the string of
islands just offshore.

The mother-otter ran a paw over her nose, the white flesh
of the healed wound still sensitive. She ignored the sting as
images of food sprang into her mind—clams and mussels,
snails and innkeeper worms, limpets and abalone. But when
she poked her head in the water to look down, she glimpsed a
favorite lurking just below her, clinging to the very bottom of
the kelp forest stipes in which she'd slept. Succulent urchins
would soon fill her belly, and his, for an hour at least.

But first, she'd have to go fishing. Though her pup was too
buoyant to sink, in preparation, she once again wrapped her

pup in protective strands of kelp, weaving them carefully into a secure cocoon that would keep him from drifting away while she dove for their morning meal.

Her small, sleek body flashed briefly in the gathering light, then bulleted to the bottom as she aimed for the orange urchins, their sharp spines no deterrent to her clever paws with their retractable claws. And her articulated fingers gave her the only hands in the ocean—other than those of the humans she sometimes encountered. Grasping an urchin, she yanked it from the kelp's holdfast, then placed it inside the skin-pocket of her left forearm, leaving plenty of room for other food or rock-tools she might need.

More. Need more. Feeding me, feeding pup.

She pulled two more urchins, brushing aside the kelp blades that undulated in the deep waves, then pushed off the bottom to swim upwards with her treasures. The moment her pup glimpsed her head breaking the surface, he began to squeal, the sound part pleasure, part urgent need. Yet she couldn't just hand him an urchin. As a two-month-old, he wasn't yet prepared to devour his own prey.

Withdrawing one urchin from her fur-sleeve, she chomped into it, using her tongue to move it from side to side between sharp teeth, then used her fingers to tear out a piece for her offspring.

With a squeal of delight, he took the treat.

Mother and pup gave one hundred percent of their focus to the repeating task of shredding and sharing, swallowing and savoring. And as they bobbed at the surface through the long morning, they lost all sense of time.

6

Doug Haliwell glanced in his rearview mirror and noted that today his hair looked almost exactly as spiky and orange as the spines on the urchin he'd soon be harvesting.

With a guff of laughter he slammed out of his truck and inhaled the sharp tang of fish and seaweed that lingered over the commercial fishing area of the Santa Barbara marina, then headed for the boat that was his second home during the season. Dru was already aboard, standing in the wheelhouse, checking gauges, tidying paperwork and stowing whatever would tend to fly off surfaces once they were under way.

Doug still wasn't entirely sure how he felt about Drusilla MacIntosh, who currently served as tender, but not for lack of qualifications, focus, or energy on the job. He just couldn't get used to the idea of a woman becoming a commercial diver, and everyone in the business knew that tenders only tended because they were determined to earn their stripes as divers. They did the boring work pre-dive, checking levels and hoses, locations and equipment. Then they did the sludge post-dive work of pulling equipment and heavily filled product baskets out of the water. Between the pre and the post, there was the monotonous waiting while they cast an intermittent gaze over empty water, wondering where and when their diver would surface. Of course, that monotony could be broken in seconds by a sudden sighting of a predator. But that seldom happened.

Some outfits were large enough that they carried a captain, crew, and divers. But for his own small company, he served as both Captain and diver, with a tender minding the boat while he was submerged. His previous tender had bailed when a better offer lured him to the Chesapeake shores, and that was when the eager "Dru" MacIntosh had shown up, long blond hair sun-bleached, white teeth blazing, sturdy body poured nicely into tight jeans, and strong-looking hands sporting short nails and no jewelry.

She'd managed to talk him into a test dive, for starters. It'd been important to Doug to get a sense of just how comfortable she was in the water. She'd asked whether an easy, local dive site would work. When he'd said yes, she'd suggested Hendry's Beach, a local favorite with easy entry down the steps from a parking lot leading to a gradually sloped sandy bottom to a depth of about thirty feet.

He'd let her lead the way as they glided over patches of rock, stands of kelp, and a decent variety of wildlife. He knew it'd be an easy dive with their SCUBA gear, and it was— except for tricky footing on some sharp rocks getting in and out, made more difficult when they had to handle the full heft of their tanks and weight belts.

There'd been no question she handled herself well under the waves, kept her equipment in good order, and had a keen eye, spotting and pointing out abalone on the sea floor, urchins on the kelp holdfasts, all while doing the occasional roll to keep aware of what critters might be swimming overhead.

After their hour's dive, they'd stowed their gear in his truck, hosed off in the parking lot, then ducked into public restrooms for a quick change of clothes. Then she'd treated him to his favorite Eggs Benedict at the Hendry's iconic Boathouse Restaurant while he'd drilled her with questions—everything from diving protocols to expectations, and from background to future plans.

Ignoring the obvious—like how great her curves looked in her wetsuit underwater, and how her smile dazzled topside—he'd catalogued her quick reflexes, surprisingly strong hands, and natural grace and power as she swam. Ultimately, he'd agreed to give her a six-month trial period, not so much because he wanted to, but because he couldn't find a good enough reason not to.

He glanced up at her now, streaked hair in a tangle down her back, tight jeans as sun-bleached as the rest of her, focused on her work in the wheelhouse. *I suppose I'll get used to having a woman aboard one of these days. Meanwhile, she's the one who's working, and I'm the one who's dawdling.*

"Morning," he called.

"Morning." She smiled down at him.

"John asked us to help him fill a big *uni* order today," he said, eager to outline their task for the day. The prized urchin sushi was a local delicacy.

"'Kay," she assented. "You've got a message from Dave, too, about your new bookkeeper needing some info."

"Oh, yeah." He'd forgotten Dave was meeting with the new person today. "I'll give him a call later, when we take a lunch break."

"Roger that," she said, returning to her tasks.

Fifteen minutes later, the *Finwell* was chugging its way out of the harbor, bound for the island of Santa Cruz.

7

Will Marks rolled his shoulders a couple of times, then stood to get another cup of coffee from the break room.

Clarke Shipping's office stood atop the bluff that gave it a view of Morro Bay with its famous rock, as well as a panorama of the larger San Luis Bay that swept in a wide arc north toward Cayucos. The cozy, smaller bay was home to marine wildlife and sport fishing, its Embarcadero a magnet for tourists, its quiet streets a respite for a thriving community from young families to retirees. The larger bay, deep enough to accommodate ocean liners and tankers, was the ideal setting for his company, founded by Russell Clarke, an illusive mogul who was seldom in residence here at headquarters.

Wishing, as he always did, that he had a sliver of ocean view from his own office, Mark stepped into the empty conference room to take a sip of coffee while savoring a glimpse of the water. No matter the color—this morning the Pacific was gray with a hint of navy blue—it always spoke to his soul and helped him to think. He was looking forward to actually being out *on* the water soon. Francine had agreed to meet him in Santa Barbara, where he'd planned a kayaking trip for them. *Haven't known her that long, but she said she loves the water. At least that'll give us one thing in common.*

The sound of a conversation pulled him away from his reverie, and he realized it was time to end his coffee break and get back to work at his desk. But as he began the short walk, he became interested in what he was overhearing.

"And he expects you to drive up outside of office hours?" It was Gladys, their office manager, speaking.

"Yes," confirmed Stacey Chernak in her European accent— German, or maybe Swiss, he wasn't sure which.

"But that means it has to be on the weekend, because it'd be dark by the time we close. And in the dark you wouldn't be able to see a thing at the house."

"Yes. The last time I was there, I had an appointment during the day with Mr. Kevin, who is in charge of construction. He was so nice. He showed me everything, answered all my questions."

"I remember you telling me about it. And didn't he make you wear a hard hat, and hold your arm so you wouldn't trip over any of the unfinished boards and wires?"

"Oh, yes, he did."

There was a moment of silence, and Mark felt awkward standing in the hallway. *Gotta either go back to my desk, or find another excuse for walking to the break room again.*

"Well, I don't like it, Stacey, I don't mind telling you. Do you want me to have a word with Mr. Clarke?"

"Oh, no!" Stacey's voice sounded shrill with fear.

"Well how about if I go with you, then?" Gladys asked.

"But . . . he did not ask for you to go, and I would not want for you to get into trouble."

"Oh, believe me, I can handle myself. And what about your husband? Doesn't he get annoyed when you're late?"

"It is true, he does not like for his dinner not to be served on time."

During the next gap in their conversation, Mark stepped toward the break room where the two women were, knowing his sudden appearance was likely to stop their talking. Now he felt conflicted. On the one hand, employees could talk about anything they liked, and it was none of his business. But on the other hand, now he'd overheard something that seemed to border on inappropriate use of an employee's time. As a Vice President of the firm, it was up to him to make sure assets and resources were used efficiently, and that time spent by employees could be justified. Mr. Clarke's personal house fell outside the responsibilities of anyone at the firm. But the man he'd have to call to account was the man who signed everyone's checks. *I hate this. Why did I eavesdrop?*

When he stepped into the room, the two women's heads snapped around and their gazes fixed on him.

"Ladies," he said.

"Something we can do for you, Mr. Marks?" Gladys asked with mock formality.

"Just getting some coffee," he answered, acutely aware that his mug was still mostly full.

"Mmm Hmm," she replied, in that expressive African-American way that indicated she wasn't buying one word of his excuse.

So Will decided to come clean. "Thought I heard you talking about Mr. Clarke's house up in Milford-Haven. You're so lucky to have seen it! I hear it's gonna be a real showplace."

Stacey's face, which a moment before had made her look like a scared rabbit about to bound away, now relaxed into a tentative smile. "It is very beautiful. Well, I mean it *will* be. When I saw it, there were only a few walls, many open holes in the structure, and it was hard to tell what would be where."

He had to focus when she spoke, because every "w" was pronounced like a "v", making it hard to understand her. "But the siting," he pressed, "it's pretty amazing, right? I mean, the view?"

"Oh my, yes, the view will be most extraordinary. Even more lovely than what we have here," she added, gesturing toward the conference room across the hall.

"Well, I gotta get back to work," Will said, effecting an exit without any grace. He closed the door to his private space and sat at his desk. *At least I didn't pretend not to have heard them at all. Theoretically, that leaves either one of them the opportunity to discuss the issue with me, if they choose to. If they don't . . . what should I do?*

His phone rang, and he handled a business call, then returned to the spreadsheet he'd been working on earlier. The ethical question still poked at the back of his mind while he worked, but in the end, he made his decision. For now, what he'd do about this issue was absolutely nothing.

8

Miranda Jones wound carefully through the curves that led down from her parental home's perch atop Belvedere Island, too busy negotiating the steep, narrow passage to let sadness pull at her.

There it is—that sentimental tug I always feel when I leave Mom. It hadn't been that long since I'd seen her. The familiar cocktail—a mix of guilt, hope, memories, expectations, and disappointments—coursed through her, doing its best to cloud her brain. Breaking it down into its component parts seemed to help keep the mixture from reaching her heart, where it was sure to cause a longing that would distract and disrupt.

The switchbacks flattened and she found herself in the small, private network of Marin's side streets, filled with short cuts and secret ways she and her sister had memorized during childhood when they'd raced these roads on their bicycles. From here, she could go north when she reached Mill Valley, turn right over the Richmond Bridge and travel south to Oakland, and continue south along the eastern shore of the long San Francisco Bay. But that seemed counter-intuitive, and she opted instead to join the 101, cross the Golden Gate, and pass through the city.

The drive south from the Bay Area to California's Central Coast—normally such a joy—shredded her patience today. From Marin, she had to navigate her way through traffic, scarcely glancing out her windows for a shutter's-beat of the breathtaking views. She'd driven these choked roads often during the two years she and Meredith had lived as roommates in their Russian Hill apartment.

Now the Marin Highlands shouldered up into her rearview mirror, ribboned by the red-slatted striations of the Golden Gate's support struts. As bridge traffic poured into downtown, she stole glances at the Financial District where her sister worked. Her office wasn't far from here—one of those glass towers that overlooked the Bay, where fingers clicked on keyboards, and money changed hands in the form of electronic numerals moving from account to account at the speed of a keystroke. *But if my office were in that tower, I'd spend the whole day gazing out the window, trying to capture the view on canvas. That sure wouldn't meet dad's idea of proper productivity quotient!*

Rising above the other structures stood the Transamerica Building in its glory, still the tallest in the city's skyline rising nearly a thousand feet. She remembered some details from the report she'd given in class during junior high. It'd been built in the early 1970s, and there was something about the truss system at its base having been designed to support both vertical and horizontal loading, carefully engineered to take large horizontal base shear forces. She knew firsthand the skyscraper proved its worth during the 1989 Loma Prieta earthquake. When the 7.1 temblor struck the Santa Cruz Mountains sixty miles from downtown, the 49-story Transamerica shook for over a minute, its top story swaying for over 12 inches from side to side. Yet the building sustained no damage and no one was seriously injured.

To her, it seemed a spectacular marriage of form and function, solidity and aery fancy, a science-fiction story about a rocket that'd pulled its wings tight enough to its body to land pointed-nose-up at the edge of a coastal city.

An impatient driver interrupted her daydream with a loud honk and a rude gesture meant as a reprimand, or worse. Suppressing the urge to retaliate with some gesture of her own, she tried to blend into southbound traffic on the 101, her face grim, her foot firmly pressed to the accelerator, until she found a niche in the flow of metal and rubber on concrete.

Now, niche established, she flowed in a high-powered energy stream of cars separated only feet from one another, and people divided from actual contact as completely as if they were in different time zones. *Maybe we are in different zones, like particles in separate quantum streams, aware of one another, but unable to communicate.*

But her science fiction reverie was soon penetrated by images from her parental visit, like flashes of an old family movie. As the images paraded by in review and were slotted into categories, she realized, with some surprise, that almost all of them were good. Granted, her dad had made his usual snide comments, but Mother had chided him and defended her.

Then there'd been that shopping trip to Gump's, something she'd frankly dreaded right up until they'd stepped through the front doors. Mom had surprised her with her astute awareness of Miranda's personal taste, her generosity in purchasing that elaborate, expensive wall unit . . . elaborate, expensive, but also perfectly coordinated with Miranda's home, something she'd have put on a wish list, if she had one. *And now it'll be delivered to my place, a gift I tried so hard to refuse.*

There's no question it was an act of generosity. But was it also a bribe? Would it be leveraged in some future negotiation? Or did it portend actual approval? *Don't know if I'd go that far. Maybe Kuyama will have an insight about it.*

The 101 streamed through San Jose, now, and as traffic began to thin, more space opened between cars. She wiggled in her seat, adjusting as tension in her back eased. The foothills of the Diablo Range rose to her left, topped by Mount Hamilton and the Lick Observatory—a collection of tiny white buildings gleaming in the sun from this distance, something she'd like to see some day. And to her right, the ocean lay just out of view, though she'd be able to see it again at Salinas. Farther south in Atascadero, her friend Kuyama would be waiting in her cozy cottage, tea ready to prepare, but it was their upcoming conversation that was already brewing.

Very Jones stood for one moment more watching the brake lights of her daughter's Mustang disappear through the gates of the family estate.

She'll catch more traffic than she wanted to . . . probably take her a good two hours just to get to San Jose. But I saw she has her music cassettes all lined up in their caddy on her passenger seat. She's so self-sufficient.

The notion caught in her throat, as it always did: her baby, all grown up, hardly in need any more of the tender ministrations a mother could offer. Her hand still in the air from performing that silly infinity-sign family wave, she morphed the gesture, now, into a dismissive one, as if to chase off the sadness that threatened to swamp her.

Drawing the tie of her robe tighter, she stepped back inside to close and lock her front door, its massive weight and size overkill now that she had no little girls to protect. Yet she still loved the home she and Charles had bought years earlier. Neither of them could imagine living anywhere else. Very had even helped to found the Belvedere Community Foundation in 1990 when she and a group of neighbors decided to honor their good fortune at living in their magnificent enclave by giving back to the community.

This two-and-a-half square mile duet of islands—of which half an acre was actually water, and on which no restaurants or stores were allowed—proved the old adage that value was all about "location, location, location," or, in this case, "view, view, view." From the south side, views went all the way from the East Bay to Sausalito and encompassed the sparkling skyline of San Francisco and the Golden Gate.

And now, her youngest had moved into some rental where all she saw was a sliver of ocean, when she had time. *But it's hers. That's all that matters to her.* Very smiled in recognition of the need, and of the accomplishment. *Wish she were buying it, building some equity. But maybe that'll come in time, too. Little does she know, I'd buy her the house, if Charles would let me.*

She smiled again, remembering Miranda's surprise and delight at the furniture gift from Gump's. *Figured I'd guessed right about what she'd like. She mentioned the re-do of her room here at home, too, said it was beautiful.*

Did children ever understand how much it meant to give them such gifts as a parent could, to have those gifts appreciated? Did they care that their parents worried about their welfare, fretted about missed opportunities, wondered where and how they might open a door, make a connection, protect from harm? Or did the care and worry just chafe and irritate, as it seemed to? *We did have some good moments, this visit, despite her frustrations.*

With a sigh, Very headed up the stairs to her bedroom to dress for the day. As she gripped the staircase, she suddenly flashed back to the banister in her own parents' home, the gracious old Victorian in the tiny town in West Virginia. She paused on the step, recalling her mother's voice, which managed to be soft and stern all at once. By six every morning, Mother had her hair in a graceful bun, tiny diamond earrings winking at her ears, crisp skirts rustling as she walked to comb her daughter's hair, pull tight the bedspread or plump the pillows.

Not only had her late mother governed her home with ironclad discipline, she'd also filled it with comforts, and taught her daughters to do the same. A gust of air from an open window pushed open the swinging door that led from the pantry, bringing with it the last traces of that distinctive cooking aroma—fresh-baked biscuits. *Is that why I asked Ana to make them this morning? Because they brought a memory of my own childhood?*

Yes, that was probably it. She'd wanted to send her own child away filled with the comfort of a memory handed down from generation to generation. *Hold it close, Miranda dear. These moments are all too fleeting.*

9

Doug Haliwell gazed at the rapidly approaching profile of Santa Cruz, the largest of the Channel Islands at over twenty miles in length. Though it offered gigantic sea caves, sandy beaches, and hiking along awesome cliff trails, he'd see none of that today—though he might spot an island fox, or a scrub jay, creatures that lived nowhere else on Earth.

Doug loved his work, how its physical rigors kept him fit, how the challenge of the ocean kept him alert and wary, how the sun and wind whipped at him as if to remind him how good it felt to be alive. Yet when he came home from the sea and wind and sun, he loved nothing better than to read. And his favorite subject was history. The endless eddies and currents of mankind's endeavors, humans' responses to circumstances—sometimes greedy, sometimes clever and, rarely, magnanimous—formed an ocean of thought he found endlessly fascinating.

He glanced at Dru, her gaze fixed on the approaching island. Normally, he'd take time to check his charts, review the location of his last urchin dive in these waters. But she'd already done all that. *Why does she have to be so efficient? And why does she have to look cute doing it?* Whether she'd intended to or not, she'd given him a few extra minutes to himself. She, like his other colleagues, had no reason to suspect his bookish side. He rarely spoke about his studies except to old teachers and classmates. For the few remaining minutes of the trip from the mainland, he indulged himself by reviewing some of what he'd read about the island.

It'd gone through several distinct chapters in its history. As early as thirteen thousand years earlier, it'd been the home of the Chumash, who'd created a complex society involving marine harvest, specialized crafts, and trade with the mainland population using the shell money they created. All that ended tragically with the arrival of Cabrillo and his Spanish settlers, who brought disease that killed thousands of the native people, then sequestered the survivors in Missions.

In its next iteration, the island became home to prisoners brought there by the Mexican government, who used it to isolate criminals. But after California passed from Mexican to American control, an English physician built the island's first ranch house, where he brought the first sheep to the island. Sheep ranching prospered during the Civil War, when the demand for wool was high. Eventually, the rancher imported cattle and horses to the island, then built roads and a wharf. In the 1930s, a large portion of the island was bought by an oilman, who switched his focus to cattle ranching. So now there was sheep ranching on one end of the land, cattle ranching on the other.

The island had at different times been home to smugglers, bootleggers and otter hunters. It'd also been an early warning outpost during World War II, and during the Cold War it housed a communications station. As far as he knew, it was still in use to some extent by the Pacific Missile Range Facility.

Meanwhile, all kinds of litigation created a political snafu when the government wanted to create the Channel Islands National Park starting in 1980. It was only at the end of 1996—just a few months ago—that government officials settled, and the way was opened for the National Park to include Santa Cruz. Even at that, other entities retained ownership of some of its real estate.

Doug dropped anchor, fastened his ball cap on its hook near the transom, and began pulling on his wet suit. There was only light chop here on the northern side of the island facing the coastline. The weather was beautiful, a cool 62 degrees—normal for February. Wet suit on, but not yet zipped, he carefully laid out the gear he'd be wearing: booties, weight belt, gloves, neoprene hood, mask.

Meanwhile, Dru had already attached his coiled yellow hose. Hookah diving—the simplest form of surface-supplied diving—consisted of a small low-pressure air compressor connected to a steel gas container. Air was pumped from the compressor into the tank, which was connected directly to the diver's breathing air hose. To prevent tension on the diver's mouthpiece, it was connected to a harness, which Doug put on next. *I didn't even have to grab it from the gear box, since she had everything laid out.*

Before putting on his mask, he glanced around the boat.

The bejeweled surface of the water sparkled out to a soft horizon, a gentle breeze blew, and the prospect of hauling up a profitable cache beckoned. But all this beauty belied the dangers that might lurk. Hunting up lucrative urchins had caused a spate of fatalities in Maine five years earlier, and Doug took the implied warnings seriously.

He'd read accounts of six deaths during 1992 and 1993—all diving for sea urchins in the waters off the coast of Maine. According to the Maine Department of Marine Resources, the U.S. Coast Guard, the Office of the Chief Medical Examiner in Maine, and the Occupational Safety and Health Administration (OSHA), each of the deaths was attributed to drowning. Doug recalled that one diver couldn't be found by his boat tender, who'd tried in vain to locate his partner in heavy fog. He was found submerged half an hour later, but CPR was unsuccessful.

If I got in trouble . . . would Dru find me in time? Would she resuscitate me? That old axiom, that you can't be too careful, is probably truer underwater than anywhere. Doug's professor at Santa Barbara City College had drilled this into all his students, and Doug had made it a practice to remember his warnings, work through his checklist, then take a moment to focus before every dive. *You never know. Today could be the day.*

Ten minutes later, Doug was over the side and sinking to the bottom, his eyes trained on the lines of orange-brown spikes that would be his target. The urchin's foot would attach like a suction cup to any number of surfaces. The holdfast of the kelp branches were its preferred spot, but today, he found them clinging to a long pipe that lay on the ocean floor. *Great! I can fill a bag or two right here. Unless an otter comes along.*

The last thing he wanted to encounter was a one of those varmints. With their sharp teeth and deadly claws, there were well equipped to snatch their favorite prey. *And they have the aggressive attitude to compete for them.*

Doug took a moment to look in every direction—including up—before using his urchin rake and going to work at popping urchins off the pipe and into his fish bag. The specialized tool always looked to him like a short, narrow metal ladder with a bangle-bracelet that fit over his forearm, and a good solid grip. He'd long since mastered the tool, but despite his heavy gloves, he still had to be careful of the needle-sharp spines when he maneuvered the creatures off their perches. A piercing through a finger would be an annoyance. It happened—it just meant cleaning the wound later to avoid infection.

In a few minutes his first bag was full, and Doug stowed his rake to free both hands. Carefully pulling closed the opening into his prey-bag, he was about to anchor it to his belt when he caught movement in the periphery of his mask. Whipping around, he was just in time to see an otter streaking past, aiming for his bag.

Oh no you don't, you bastard. These are mine.

Drawing his bag closer, Doug bent his knees and shoved off the bottom to begin his ascent. He glanced at his watch to check his dive-time, careful not to surface too quickly, but the otter was already swiping at his bag.

And then the otter performed a sleek backward somersault, revealing its underside. *Oh, hell. A nursing mother.* He didn't have the heart to hurt a mother trying to get food for her pup. *Can't fight fair unless it's man to man*, he thought, anthropomorphizing the creature despite his avowed determination to avoid doing so.

The mother otter didn't like the stick, and seemed to fear it. *Smart. She must have encountered fishermen before.* Breaking off her attack on Doug's bag, she flowed downward toward the pipe where he knew she'd find plenty of delicacies for herself and her young.

Too bad she won't devour the whole urchin. She'll tear it apart, take what she wants, and let the rest drift back to the bottom. But then, he sometimes did the same thing himself, checking to see the urchins he hoped to take to market were "full," not empty. *We all gotta make a living*, he thought, heading for the surface.

10

Kuyama Freeland sat perfectly still at the conference table, considering what their opponent had said, and what she would say in return.

The Tribal Council had agreed to one more meeting with this developer, the man who proposed building a shopping center on land sacred to her people. He claimed to have the support of the Paso Robles Chamber of Commerce, but she knew that support was far from unanimous. Now, before she could speak, the tribal lawyer spoke instead—or rather, shouted. *Poor Sisquoc only seems to have one setting: loud. But perhaps he comes by his stubbornness honestly,* she thought. *His name means "stopping place," and he's good at drawing a line in the sand.*

"We should stop for today," she said, summoning the voice of authority that sometimes surprised even her.

People on both sides of the table, faces still twisted in

anger, rose and filed out. After reassuring Sisquoc—known outside the tribe as Stephen—that a few inches of progress had been made, Kuyama climbed into her car, started the motor and checked the clock on the dashboard. She would just have time to bake Miranda's favorite biscuits and put on some water for tea.

An hour later, Kuyama was sitting at her kitchen table watching her guest drizzle honey into her steaming mug of Earl Gray.

"How was it to be with your parents?" Kuyama watched the face of her young friend closely, noticing a range of emotions cross her features like a grouping of clouds tracing across the sky.

"It went fine. My mother and I had one of our days . . . shopping, lunching, beauty salon."

"Days like that are precious, Miranda. More significant than we sometimes realize. Until later."

Miranda stirred her tea. "I know you're right. I just . . . it's not to be . . . she doesn't really see—"

"The hardest thing for a mother is to see her child as something other than her child. I often made the same mistake."

Miranda's head came up sharply. "You?"

"All of us must learn." That brought the smile Kuyama had been waiting for. "You and your mother are finding your way. I know that because you spent a whole day doing things that pleased her. That was your gift to her. And hers to you."

The younger woman sat in the stillness, apparently letting these thoughts sink in. Wind riffled through the orange tree just coming into bloom outside, sending its delightful aroma in through the kitchen window, and a robin began to sing.

As if in explanation, Kuyama said, "It's much warmer here than it is on the coast. The animals always know."

Right on cue, Atishwin walked in, his nails clicking lightly on the hardwood floor of the tidy kitchen. He looked up at Kuyama, the intelligence evident in his gaze.

"Yes, we were talking about you."

"Mm-mm," he whined.

"Would you like a treat?"

His expressive whine clearly indicated that he would, and his front paws came off the floor in a little bounce. Kuyama gathered her long skirt and walked the two steps to the cupboard to retrieve two dog treats, then handed them to Atishwin, who sat obediently before her hand opened. When Kuyama returned to her chair, she saw that Miranda was staring up at the wall where one of her own paintings hung.

"So kind of you to hang it in your home."

"Kind? Hah! That's funny. What you've given me is a window to the ocean. And no one up here in these mountains has that view, unless they have a big bankroll."

Miranda chuckled. "Well, I'm just glad you like it."

"There is another view I'd like to have some day," Kuyama offered.

"Good, I'm taking commissions these days."

"It's that view from the 46."

Miranda's gaze shifted as though she might be able to see it from where she sat, then she said, "I know exactly! As you drive west, there's a big turnout on the other side of the road, where the ocean is framed by the mountains."

"It's both past and present for me. I can see my former home, Morro Bay, but from a different altitude. From up here in the mountains, I can see things I couldn't see before." As she heard herself say the words, Kuyama recognized the spiritual truth of the insight, which meant she hadn't really thought of it herself, but was experiencing a shared moment with Spirit.

She inhaled deeply as if to take the inspiration literally, breathed out a sigh, then studied her young guest, whose silent alertness meant that she, too, had felt the Presence. That was good. Knowing Miranda had that awareness, Kuyama would worry less. "It's very beautiful," she said, to break the silence.

Miranda nodded. "I've thought about painting it several times. Now I'll move it up the list."

"And I have something for you, as well."

"Oh, there's no need to—"

But Kuyama had already reached for a book, which she handed to her friend.

"*Island of the Blue Dolphins*," Miranda read, flipping the small paperback to examine the cover and description.

"It may give you insights into the places you'll be visiting. My people came from the Channel Islands."

"Right!"

"The story is made up, but the author did good research. It seemed appropriate."

"So thoughtful! Thank you."

Kuyama nodded, and knew the time for their visit was drawing to a close. The girl had a full schedule, and had to get back on the road. "This has been wonderful." She extended both her hands, which Miranda took in her own, the fingers long and graceful, the grip firm.

"I always love being with you. Thanks for making the time."

The two women rose to give each other a fond embrace. They stood equal in height, and drew back to gaze eye to eye. Then Miranda was gone, and Kuyama was waving from her front porch. *It won't be the easiest path, but she will do much good. And I think someday will have much joy. Hope I'm still here to see it.*

Miranda Jones slowed to exit the 101 for the smaller California Highway 46, which would take her to the coast. The beautiful road wound through the vineyards of Paso Robles, then climbed through a mountain pass until it crested at a 1500-foot–high lookout, where she usually pulled off on the wide stretch of gravel provided for drivers who didn't want to miss the vista. Today, her pause at the overlook would be both pleasure and assignment.

Her tires crunched on the gravelly schist until she came to a stop, and she pushed open the driver's side door, then stood to stretch her legs. Inhaling a gulp of fresh mountain air, she squeezed her eyes shut for a moment, as if to clear them of the traffic, dotted white lines, and rear ends of trucks that'd filled her vision before arriving at Kuyama's. When she opened her eyes to the one-hundred-eighty–degree visa of rolling foothills and shining ocean stretched out in front of her, she smiled until her face ached, and hugged herself in welcome pleasure tinged with relief.

Of course she loves this spot as much as I do. I'd love to do a painting for her! What did she say? A new perspective . . . past and present. There'd been something wistful when Kuyama shared that, and then . . . something else. *Almost as if someone else came into the room. There was a presence. But big and beneficent, not ghostly or menacing.*

As an Elder of the Chumash people, Kuyama went through life with a sense of sacred purpose. Beyond that, Miranda didn't know any specifics, and had always trusted Kuyama would share with her whatever seemed appropriate. Today she's shared so much—spoken, and silent. And she'd made a request. These were so few and far between, Miranda had to assume it was significant. She would indeed place this new commission higher up her list, even though it would bring no monetary gain.

Returning her focus to the vista, she took some mental notes. *Sky and water by Turner*, she thought, as the iconic British painter's exquisite seascapes began to play through her mind like a private slide show. She tried to imagine how she herself would paint the panorama now arrayed in front of her. For the first few minutes of her reverie, paint and canvas seemed far too crude a set of tools by which to even begin to capture such grandeur. Yet as the shapes and colors began to seep into her, it seemed the universe itself was melting into virtual paint that poured itself into her heart and mind.

Sha-ha, she heard herself whisper—that private word she used to describe the indescribable, these moments that transcended the five senses and turned into "flow," a place without time or limitation where Creation poured through her like water through a stream, or light through a window.

She never analyzed these moments, for there was no point in trying to fit the infinite into the finite. Instead, she trusted this private process, knew her cauldron of colors and ideas was being filled, and also knew she would draw upon this rich storehouse in the days and weeks ahead when she'd be painting.

As if her private audience was coming to a close, Miranda felt a chill, and zipped her fleece higher. She smiled again and silently thanked the Presence for this latest gift, then climbed back into her car. Though she hadn't noticed it till now, she realized the orange of the sun was deepening, now, as the orb sank lower toward the ocean. The road that wound down to Highway 1 would be bathed in peach-colored light as she made her way home to Milford-Haven.

11

Burt Ostwald saw with relief that it was quitting time on the job site. Since last winter, he'd worked as a temp for Sawyer Construction in Milford-Haven—the nowheres-ville town where his *real* boss, Russell Clarke, was having a house built for himself. Well, given its immense size, this was hardly a "house" and would hardly be for "himself." But hey, the guy was richer than God and could build whatever the hell he wanted to build.

Burt looked around the living room, casting only a quick glance at the completed fireplace, its raised hearth now sealing off the wide opening that'd once led to the basement. *That's where I met Chris Christian. Best not to think about that right now.* Men were putting away tools, clearing up some of the debris from completed tasks. Their supervisor, Kevin Ransom, seemed a nice enough guy—unassuming, mild-mannered. But Burt had noticed the man didn't miss much. *Tall, lanky, and*

eagle-eyed. Best stay on his good side, and steer clear whenever
possible.

So as not to be seen hanging around after the rest of the
crew had left, he shuffled out with the others, gave a quick nod
to Kevin, and walked out to his truck. With some relief, he saw
the profile of the magnificent home disappearing in his rear
view mirror. But now he had a new worry.

Why, exactly, did Mr. Clarke want to see him? Or was it, in
fact, Clarke himself with whom he'd be meeting? Having never
met the man in person, how would he know for sure? Men like
him—powerful, unscrupulous, and wrapped carefully in lay-
ers of corporate paperwork—could always get their minions
to do his bidding.

He himself was a case in point. He'd been planted at the
Clarke house construction site. He'd also been told to get rid of
a little problem, which he thought he'd done with neat, clean
dispatch, not to mention discretion. He'd heard indirectly,
though, that there'd been some grumbling. Was it possible
he'd misinterpreted his orders? Was he only supposed to have
scared the woman off, rather than off-ing her all together? If
so, nothing could be done about it now—except keeping himself on his toes and being prepared for any and everything.

Burt made a quick stop at the campsite where he kept a
small portion of his gear—just enough to get by on this temp
job. He grabbed his laundry—he'd find a laundromat somewhere during his weekend travels—then zipped tight his tent,
knowing that even if the whole of these belongings were sto-
len, it'd be no great loss.

Then he began his drive south. His meeting would take
place in Santa Barbara. *Too rich for my blood. I'll find a cheap*

motel in Gaviota. Too bad I won't have time for any female com-panionship. That kind of distraction would be unwise.

What he planned to do with his time while he waited for the meet was to polish his ocean skills, and what he had in mind specifically was taking a kayak trip out toward Point Conception. That stretch of coastline beyond Gaviota was pretty much deserted, thanks to the steep cliffs that plunged into the sea. He could use the exercise and he looked forward to the challenge.

Though he didn't expect trouble, he always carried some kind of weapon. For this excursion, he'd decided on his pellet gun. Quieter and lighter than regular firearms, and often carried on boats to defend against nuisance animals, he could claim it as a "normal" piece of gear if he were ever questioned.

When he got to Santa Barbara, he'd locate a kayak rental company. He'd make it a mini-vacation. It was long overdue.

12

Miranda pressed the remote fastened to her visor and paused, the Mustang engine rumbling, until the garage door opened enough to let her park the car inside. At the very idea of being home, she could feel her shoulders drop. *Too bad I won't be here more than a night. Gotta get unpacked and repacked, then head down to Santa Barbara. Two trips, one right after the other. Yet they couldn't be more different*, she reflected.

Even though she'd been savoring the tender sense of connection with her mother, she had to acknowledge that visiting her parents always seemed to include a certain amount of unwelcome drama born of the mistaken belief—on the part of her folks, not herself—that *they* were still responsible for their younger offspring and capable of influencing her major decisions. Meredith didn't seem to experience these intrusions on the same level. So had Miranda herself somehow encouraged them to believe she was incapable of managing her own career? Was this all about their unacknowledged urge to make sure there would be grandchildren to carry on the Jones family tradition? Not entirely, because that would be aimed at Meredith too. *But that must figure in somehow*, Miranda thought.

Things were different with Mom, this time, though, she admitted. *Better. I actually think we had a breakthrough. That is, until her parting words were that I should do something with my hair. So . . . complicated. And now, here I sit in the dark in my garage, like an idiot.*

She climbed out, hefted her duffle from the Mustang's trunk, then shoved open the door that led inside from the garage. She took a moment to inhale the familiar aroma of home. *Slightly musty from having all the doors and windows closed . . . with a tinge of melted citrus candle mixed in.*

Putting first things first, she turned on some lights and slid open the door to her balcony, as well as the kitchen window, creating an instant cross breeze redolent of eucalyptus and pine. Then she set about an efficient list of tasks. Half an hour later, her washing machine's agitator had already gone to work on the laundry she'd extricated from her duffle, and the bag itself was now spread out on Miranda's still-made bed, ready to receive clothing selections for Santa Barbara. The jeans, T-shirts and jeans jacket she typically wore for her outdoor research excursions were no-brainers, and she placed these inside, along with a stack of fresh underwear, socks, and one pair of pantyhose. *Hate those things, but I better have some in case I have a nice dinner at the Calvins . . . or somewhere else in town.*

Though she'd lived in Milford-Haven for only fourteen months, she marveled how quickly she'd adapted. Now it seemed like a chore to dress appropriately for the much swankier city of Santa Barbara. Zelda would be horrified if Miranda didn't have the obligatory little-black-dress to pull on at a moment's notice—but of course, Zelda wouldn't be home. *Still, better to have the dress, just in case.*

She pushed through the hangers in the closet till she found it—the little *green* dress that'd become her default. It was Meredith who'd gifted her with a green dress first—long and sinuous, her sister's present was crafted of silk that floated over her long limbs. *Fantastic, when I have access to an iron. But not good for travel.* To find a sturdier replacement, Miranda'd asked for help from Kathy, who owned The Place in the nearby town of Cambria. Not only was the store always filled with unique garments that looked like wearable art, Kathy also had a knack for finding special things for her regular customers. Miranda could scarcely call herself a regular, but ever since she'd done a painting for the shop's wall, she found herself the recipient of discounts and deals. When Kathy found her a dark green dress made of rayon—slinky, gracefully draped, and virtually indestructible—Miranda bought two: one long-sleeved, one sleeveless, both hitting just below the knee. Miranda grabbed the dress with sleeves and rolled it into her duffle.

Her former life in San Francisco had afforded her the opportunity to dress in everything from paint-splattered overalls to crisp linens to elegant silks, when she and her sister were commanded to attend one of their mother's elegant ballet soirees. Very Jones was a mover and shaker in the world of Bay Area arts, and she expected her daughters to follow in her philanthropic footsteps. What she did *not* expect was that any daughter of hers would actually plant her feet on the artist's path herself.

Miranda's approval rating had notched up a couple of points as her own paintings had begun to bring her some success in the city's indie-arts scene. At that point, the young painter had been living in San Francisco, sharing a condo with her sister Meredith. While her investment-advisor sibling had been making good, steady money as a junior employee at Bear Stearns, Miranda had been sharing studio space with the Bays-Art Cooperative, which was a combination multiple artists' studio and gallery. Granted, during their monthly shows their guests had had to put up with the smell of turpentine and linseed oil. But most of the Co-op members had also begun to develop a following, none more successfully than the younger Ms. Jones.

She'd come to the attention of Zelda McIntyre, an upscale and, it later proved, very demanding artist's representative, whose client Miranda had become shortly after they met. Zelda, with uncanny parallels to Mrs. Very Jones, had pushed and pulled, organized and networked, until all the attention had made Miranda's head spin and her heart heavy. Her work had begun to suffer and her feeling of being inauthentic had put her in danger of believing her own press. All this had led Miranda to take a fateful drive south along California's famous Highway 1, when she'd first found the little town of Milford-Haven. Now it was home—much to the ongoing consternation of parents, artist's rep, and even sister, to some extent.

Miranda took a breath and looked down at her suitcase, where most of what she needed was now carefully packed. *I'll keep my new red dress hung in its Gump's bag. Have to pack heels for the Zoo gala, and figure out a hair clip.*

She stepped out of her bedroom to look upward along the open staircase, where the new piece of furniture would rest when it arrived. *I'll have to ask Kevin if he can come over, help me assemble it . . . unless the Gump's delivery guys will do that for me. Probably not, though.* She imagined the gleaming wood, how it would coordinate with the wood floor molding, then flow upward toward the hardwood floors on the main floor. *Wow, it'll be beautiful. I can hardly believe it'll really happen.* It would be her first truly grown-up piece of furniture, she reflected. *Well, I'm ready for it.* And that made her smile.

She walked up the stairs and took a moment to look around the open living-dining-kitchen area with its wall of sliding glass that faced a pine forest, the only barrier between the house and the sparkling blue ocean winking between the dark brown tree trunks. Her décor was such a contrast to her family's home that she laughed out loud. *I always assumed Mother would be aghast if she knew I hadn't moved here with one of her French antiques. I left them all with Meredith, who adores them.*

Her own furnishings were simple and comfortable: a chocolate brown couch was dotted with multiple pillows in various shades from chocolate to vermillion. On shelves and side tables—just as her mother had known—stood pieces of her own homemade pottery; she'd hung the high walls with her own paintings of local landscapes and seascapes. *It's coming along very nicely.*

She supposed she ought to make some dinner, then suffered a pang at missing her kitty. But dragging her home for just one night, then leaving her again, had seemed unkind. And she knew Shadow was in kitty-heaven staying as the guest of her second-favorite human, Kevin, himself something of an animal-whisperer.

The refrigerator was as starkly bare as she'd ever seen it. *That's good. No moldering food growing a bacteria garden in there.* She opened the freezer instead, where she found a hand-labeled zip-lock bag that promised spinach ravioli, made only a month earlier. That and a small jar of Alfredo sauce would do nicely, so she put a pot of water on to boil.

When she finished her meal and cleaned up the kitchen, Miranda headed for her studio, where she began gathering her research materials. Her time in Santa Barbara would be spent working on two different projects: one, a painting of sea otters commissioned by Sea Otter Rescue in Santa Barbara; the other, a project for Zelda, who wanted her to paint a mural in her newly constructed third-floor apartment.

Both projects sparked her imagination, and in such different ways. *One's a landscape, and one's a critter portrait of one of my favorites.* Between the two works, she'd have been hard pressed to choose which she preferred, so she felt grateful she didn't have to forego either. Spending a moment visualizing what each might look like, she realized the two images were melding in her mind: creature and context, coastal ocean and one of its inhabitants. *I wonder whether I could sneak a small otter into Zelda's seascape. It would fit perfectly, after all. So would a whale tail, a harbor seal, some sea stars, urchins, and abalones on rocks in the foreground. But . . . I'm getting ahead of myself. In any case, I have no doubt I'll paint a third piece for myself, once I get close to the sea otters.*

Miranda knew about the creatures anecdotally, having watched them along the Central Coast shorelines as they floated in kelp, cracked open shells on their chests, and blinked from adorable faces as they seemed to show off for the audiences of humans who often gathered to observe their antics.

What she needed to do was gather the research files she'd collected so far on the species *Enhydra lutris*, otherwise known as the California or Southern Sea Otter. She knew what text books catalogued about the marine mammal: that it was native to the coasts of the North Pacific Ocean; that adults typically weighed between 14 and 45 kg, making them the heaviest members of the weasel family, but among the smallest marine mammals; that the male lived about fifteen years, the female about ten, and that, unlike its ocean going mammalian cousins, it had no blubber to keep its body warm but relied entirely on its dense, luxurious coat. Indeed, their pelts were made of the thickest, softest, warmest fur imaginable, and by far the most dense, with millions of hairs. The price they paid was constant grooming: unless the pelt was constantly cleaned, oils reduced its function. Even with this diligence, otters spent their lives trying to stay warm, as in the 35- to 50-degree waters of the Pacific, they lost heat twenty-five times faster than they would on dry land.

She'd learn so much more on this job—both academically from the reading materials Katy, the director of S.O.R., would provide; and from the adventure of observing them close-up, an adventure that would begin to unfold as soon as she arrived in Santa Barbara.

The hour had grown late, she realized, and she needed to get a good night's sleep. Arranging her supplies at one end of her desk, she left the task of packing them for the morning, and headed downstairs to her solitary bedroom.

13

Katy Sails twisted her key to unlock the offices of SOR, leaving the door open behind her to allow the fresh sea breeze to sweep through the two small rooms. A smile tugged at her mouth as her gaze lingered on her desk plaque: Director, Sea Otter Rescue. The title sounded exalted, but the organization was, in fact, a small branch of the Monterey Bay Aquarium's otter program. Still, she loved her job and took it seriously.

The other thing she loved was the office location. In the heart of the Santa Barbara Marina, tucked into the long, narrow buildings fitted to the pier, it was rustic and simple, cozy and practical. Every professional resource she might need was within walking distance: the Waterfront Department, the Coast Guard, the Outdoors Visitor Center, the Maritime Museum, as well as various sport and boat chartering outfits. Even the Fish Market was nearby.

The whole of the Santa Barbara Harbor was a picturesque boating haven, a magnet for both neophytes and experts that sometimes created the incongruous appearance of world-class yachts docked alongside commercial fishing vessels. But this had been the case since the 1139-slip harbor was built in 1929, so it obviously worked. A short distance away, the iconic Stearns Wharf had been there even longer. Built in 1872, it was now California's oldest working wooden wharf and offered plenty of restaurants and souvenir shops. The area was crowded with visitors during the summer months. But on a lovely, chill spring morning like this, Katy relished the quiet.

She sat at her desk for a few minutes. Looking through her schedule, she made a mental note that she'd be meeting with the artist Miranda Jones later today. Katy'd received the go-ahead to hire Miranda to create a mural on the SOR wall—both a marketing practicality and an aesthetic coup, as far as she was concerned, and she looked forward to meeting her in person. Next, she reviewed current cases before she headed to the enclosure to check on current otter residents being tended by staff members.

The goal of SOR was to rescue and rehabilitate otters who'd been injured, releasing them back into the wild when they were strong enough to resume the intensive gathering and feeding regimen they needed to stay alive. But otter pups were tricky. Depending on their age, they sometimes required long-term care. And, since they'd likely be at risk in the open ocean, every effort was made to pair them with adoptive otter mothers.

Currently they were housing a rescued sea otter pup found right off the coast of Santa Barbara when she was just one day old, and weighing only about three pounds. The staff was monitoring her twenty-four hours a day, making sure she got the care a newborn needed. But what would be the fate of their small charge?

When Katy took the five-minute walk to the otter facility, she heard the mewing the moment she stepped into the enclosure. And there she was, their most adorable resident, Baby Lulu, now seven weeks old and weighing in at seven pounds.

Katy's hands itched to hold the baby, touch its soft fur and feel her heart beat through the tiny body. But human hands never touched baby otters, lest they interfere with their chance to bond with an adoptive parent. So instead, workers wore nitrile gloves when they fed the infants with specially designed bottles.

Ashley glanced up at Katy as she walked in. "You want to do the swim?" she asked when she'd finished feeding Lulu.

"May I?"

"All yours."

Katy pushed her hands into another set of gloves, then gently lifted Lulu, whose alert eyes gazed into those of her human handler. "Ready to get into the water? Yes, yes, you like the water, remember?" Katy continued to coo at her tiny charge, carrying her to the bathinet-like tub of chilly seawater, then slowly lowering her into the salty bath.

The moment the water touched Lulu's fur, the baby cried with an uncannily human sound.

"I know, I know, it's different, and scary, but you'll like it in just a minute, I promise."

Lulu kicked her webbed feet and blinked, still uncertain of this new element. Katy dribbled water across one arm, then the other, and Lulu's cries became less desperate. Then, a tiny hand reached out to pat the water, and her sweet face showed both surprise and delight when it splashed.

"What a smart girl you are," Katy praised. "Yes, such a smart girl. And you'll be a great swimmer one day, you'll see." Katy brought the baby to the warming table, where she carefully dried her with a towel, then delivered her back to Ashley who would check her vitals before arranging her next feeding.

"Such fun, isn't it?" Ashley said.

"Oh, she's precious. I get so attached," Katy added wistfully.

"Wish we could teach her everything she needs to know."

"To survive in the wild? How I wish," Katy agreed. "Okay, thanks, Ashley. See you later."

As Katy headed back to her office, she couldn't help but feel sad there was even a need for this rescue facility, yet enough baby and adult otters were found either injured or oil-damaged, that it was certainly warranted.

She feared little Lulu would never swim free, never dive the deep kelp beds for her food, or float on the tide with a raft of relatives. She'd have a good life—they'd see to that. But it might be a life lived in captivity.

14

Dave Dax stood under the dockside shower letting the water cool his body. Today he'd kept to a moderate pace, completing three miles in just over a half hour. During competition, he could finish a 5K in fifteen minutes, but for normal workouts he didn't push it that hard.

Today he'd decided to run along Cabrillo, its oceanside track an attraction for tourists later in the day, and for locals early in the morning. In his peripheral vision he enjoyed seeing the Pacific's straight blue horizon. And while he ran, he'd kept an eye on fellow runners in case he saw Sandra. *Not today. Guess she ran somewhere else, if she ran at all.*

Before his shower, he'd checked on their three boats bobbing in their slips. Now he switched off the water then stepped to one side, where he'd balanced a clean towel on his running shoes. Now he pressed the thirsty terrycloth around his soaked running shorts, which he knew would be almost dry by the time he arrived at the office, where he always kept a set of clean clothes.

Ten minutes after he arrived at D&D Channel Charters, he had the coffee machine burbling and the computer booting, and figured he was ready for the day to begin. And it did when the phone rang—right on time.

"D&D Charters," he answered cheerily.

"Yeah, I wanted to ask about renting a boat for a harbor tour, then maybe taking it a little farther up the coast?"

"I can help you with that," he replied smoothly, beginning his spiel about tours, guides, and equipment. Twenty minutes later, he'd taken a deposit from a San Diego couple visiting Santa Barbara for a few days.

He typed up the order, and while it was printing, the phone rang again.

"D&D Charters."

"Hi. It's Sandra."

"Hey." He smiled and cradled the phone with his shoulder. "Looked for you this morning."

"Running? I was up on the Mesa running a trail this morning."

"Love it up there."

"Yeah. You know where I want to go one of these days? Out to the Ventura River Preserve," she offered. "I hear it's so peaceful. It'd be a nice change of pace."

"It would," he agreed, "when you have to make the hour-drive to Ojai."

"Exactly. I usually don't go that far."

The phone rang, interrupting their congenial chat. "Can you hold a second?"

"Sure," she said.

"D&D Charters."

"Hi," a man's voice began. "I wonder if you could give me some information about a kayak excursion?"

"Absolutely. Let me just wrap up another call and I'll be right back to you."

"Okay."

"Sandra? Sorry . . . gotta take this call from a customer. May I call you back a little later?"

"Sure," Sandra said. "I had a couple more questions. Any time is fine."

"Thanks." Dave depressed the button for the second line on his phone. *Fun talking to her. Maybe we could have a drink or something. . . .*

"Hello? Okay, I'm back." Dave took a breath, switching back to professional-mode. "You were asking about a kayak rental? Can I get your name?"

Once again Dave outlined options for his prospective client. This one wanted to travel along the coastline out toward Point Conception in hopes of spotting some wildlife, sea otters in particular. Dave spent a good half hour on the phone, helping him to plan a day of adventure, a short oceanic photo safari, lunch included.

Before he hung up, he completed the order for a man named Will Marks.

15

ill Marks hung up the phone, pleased with the plans for a day on the water with his girlfriend. He opened the narrow utility closet in his apartment to pull out his vacuum. He'd already wiped down the bathroom and kitchen counters, started a load in the dishwasher, and changed the sheets on his bed. A few quick strokes with the Hoover would complete his efforts at tidying up before his trip to Santa Barbara. His regular cleaning crew came every two weeks and did a thorough job. But he disliked returning home from a weekend to find mess left over from the previous work week. Now, he surveyed his work. *Not the greatest job, but not bad*, he told himself, wrapping the cord and replacing the unit in the closet.

Francine Mackie—who flew for the small-but-growing Western Pacific Airline—had a four-day turnaround this time, which would give them a chance to get to know each other better. They hadn't decided yet whether they'd drive up to Morro Bay and spend a night or two right here in his apartment, or whether they'd just enjoy themselves at their hotel in Santa Barbara. He hoped for the latter, but wanted to be prepared just in case. *Nothing like used sheets and a dirty kitchen to put a woman off.*

They'd met on one of his business flights, when she'd caught his eye while serving drinks in First Class—such as it was on a small aircraft. Pert and pretty, she'd also been calm and steady when they hit turbulence. She had a grace about her as she went through the motions of serving and assisting passengers. *Not sure what it was exactly, but she sure captured my interest. And she has a nice voice. After listening to Randi's rants, the voice thing is a must.*

Several weeks earlier, Will had ended the on-again-off-again relationship he'd had with the radio announcer Randi Raines, a woman who'd certainly known exactly how to "rain" on his plans. He'd taken her to the little town of Milford-Haven north of Morro Bay, and she thought it a backwater. Ironically, it was Santa Barbara where she'd love to have spent a weekend. But he now knew her goal would have been to see and be seen, rather than to get to know him. She'd been steamy between the sheets—except when she'd had too much to drink, which had grown more and more often. He'd felt a great sense of relief when she'd agreed they should stop seeing each other. *Lessons learned. Better luck this time. A man can hope.*

Then, a few weeks ago, when Will had made a quick round trip to the Bay Area for meetings, he'd waited inside the terminal, waited till the flight crew exited the plane. Francine had spotted him and broken away from her colleagues.

"Something I can help you with?" she'd asked, her head

cocked to one side, somehow striking just the right balance between flirtatious and professional.

"I hope so," he'd replied, sounding more confident than he'd felt. "I was wondering whether you have dinner plans?"

"Dinner in San Jose tonight, but I'll be back in Santa Barbara Thursday."

"Thursday's good."

"Okay. A bright, open place with lots of people and it has to be Dutch treat. Okay?"

Now it'd been his turn to smile. "Okay. How about meeting at the Paseo off State Street?"

"That'll work. I can be there by seven."

The butterflies in his stomach had gradually settled as he'd driven himself the two hours north to Morro Bay that evening.

The following Thursday, that first dinner date had been casual, fun, and relaxed. He'd enjoyed their slow stroll down State Street, the easy way they shared war-stories about their jobs, movies they loved and hated, travels they longed to enjoy or never wanted to repeat. Light from the street lamps played on her gold-brown hair, which ruffled in the sea breezes when they walked out onto the Pier. They ended that first evening with her standing on tiptoe to kiss his cheek, though he'd wanted more, even then.

They handled that all-important question on their second date.

"When do you want to have sex?" she asked at dinner, and he nearly spat his bite of fish across the table. She giggled at his reaction, laughed harder when she saw his blush.

"Would now work?" he asked, when he stopped choking.

They skipped dessert and coffee and headed for her place, a condo in a complex near the beach in Carpenteria. The place was not unlike his own, which was just two hours north, also close to the water. Where his place was decorated mostly in marine blue, hers was white and beige, with huge pillows, comfortable furniture and an impressive collection of shells placed on tables, shelves, and a mantle over a gas fireplace. *Our stuff would go together easily*, he thought, then wondered where the hell that idea had come from.

He failed to notice any of the details in her bedroom, because all his focus was on her. He'd peeled away the V-neck sweater and the tight jeans before she could, revealing creamy skin that vibrated at his touch. She'd returned the favor, apparently enjoying what she saw when she drew off his shirt, undid his pants and let his jeans fall to the floor.

Hungry as they were for each other, he'd done his best to slow down enough to savor this first intimacy, pleasure her first, ask the right questions, move forward without making assumptions. He knew from her responses that she enjoyed herself, enjoyed him. From the start, they were two people communicating with, not just consuming, each other. *That sure made a change from being with Randi. I used to feel like I was dinner, not a dinner date.*

The next morning, they knew they were having fun. Enough fun, that they'd looked at their calendars and, miraculously, found a time when they could both take a long weekend. Will hadn't taken time off since last Christmas, and he had a lot of sick days stored up. Francine had flown extra routes for two of her pals, so she had time off coming, too.

Now they were coming up to their fifth date, comfortable with each other, and ready for the next adventure. Still, how would they fare stuck in a tiny boat, he wondered. She did have experience on the water—at least as much as he did, having grown up near Lake Tahoe. Would she insist on doing everything herself, or was she a team player? How would she do in a crisis? *Fine. She's a flight attendant! I bet she can handle whatever comes up. In fact, I'm counting on it. Not that anything bad will happen.*

16

Miranda Jones pulled up to a stoplight and glanced once more at the map on her passenger seat. Folded to reveal only the downtown area of Santa Barbara, its red marker line reminded her where to turn for Zelda's home.

Actually, for Zelda it was both home and business, she reminded herself—a small complex with a storefront on the ground floor and her elegant apartment on the second and third floors, with a small balcony overlooking its own court-yard, in which Miranda had enjoyed painting the *trompe l'oeil* jasmine vines winding upwards from real pots planted at intervals.

When the car behind her honked, she glanced in her rearview mirror, waved an apology, and pressed on toward the upcoming turn into Zelda's *porte-cochère*, where a valet awaited. Since self parking wasn't an option, Miranda pulled to a stop and smiled as the liveried employee opened her car door.

"Good afternoon, Miss," he said in a Hispanic accent.

"Good afternoon. I'm here at the invitation of Ms. McIntyre, I'm—"

"Ah, you are Miss Miranda Jones. We have been expecting you."

"Well, thank you."

"I am Ramon. I will help you while you stay with Mrs. Z. Just let me know what you would like me to bring upstairs. I will park for you, and bring your luggage."

"I have rather a lot, I'm afraid. I brought painting supplies."

"This is no problem, Miss."

The smile lit the man's round, swarthy face, and Miranda couldn't have avoided smiling back if she'd tried.

Half an hour later, Ramon had finished helping Miranda haul her duffle, easel, paint bag, and hanging bag from the elevator, across the marble foyer and into Zelda's guest room. He then gave her a set of keys and a list of codes and instructions, and showed her the food he'd been instructed to order in for her. Then, refusing the modest tip Miranda offered, he excused himself and left by the front door.

Miranda sighed and glanced around the town home. Though it hadn't been many months since her last visit, the place seemed different without its owner being present, and Miranda found herself noticing details she'd overlooked before.

It wasn't till she'd completed her self-tour that she spotted Zelda's note on the kitchen counter.

Dear Miranda

Welcome. I would say I'm sorry not to be here in person, but actually this is ever so much better, as you'll be able to paint in peace without my complaining about fumes. As we've already discussed, I'm giving you a free hand in the little upstairs apartment. The only thing I require is that you bring the outside, inside, in that lovely trompe l'oeil *style you used for my courtyard. I do like unification of design, and think some kind of faux window view upstairs will be just the thing to complete the space. As you'll see, the cabinet maker did a masterful job, and I think your idea to hire a boat builder was a stroke of genius. Hope you agree.*

I'm only a phone call away should you need me. Have fun, eat all the food, and do work hard, so it's all finished before I get home. Ta ta, Zelda

Miranda laughed out loud at Zelda's ability to sound both brusque and supportive in print, just as she could in person. She really was like no one else. Maddening as her bossiness could sometimes be, Miranda knew her to have the best of intentions, and the smartest of ideas, too. *So much like Mother in some ways. Did I miss Mom so much that I looked for a surrogate to keep close? Or is it just that my unresolved mother-issues are following me everywhere I go?*

Leaving that question to one side, Miranda could no longer suppress her curiosity. *I've got to see this little upstairs room. Never even knew it existed!* For a moment, she couldn't locate stairs that would lead up. Then, she spotted an "invisible" door—a section of wall whose wainscoting matched that of the rest of the room. Walking over, she pressed on what appeared to be a wall-section, and felt a gentle snick as it opened toward her. "Wow!" she said out loud. "Like a French chateau!"

Light from above illuminated the narrow set of stairs, which she climbed till she arrived at a full-floor room with upper walls angling up to a peak. A skylight let in streaks of afternoon sun, and dormer windows brought still more sun and space into the area.

The quarters were framed and sheetrocked, with the lower halves of the walls finished in gleaming cabinetry. The stairs accessed one end of the apartment, which held a tiny kitchenette, and in one of the dormer window openings stood a café table with two chairs. The next area was delineated by partial walls that formed a cozy living area with a scaled-down sectional sofa—still wrapped in factory plastic sheeting—that faced an ingeniously constructed wall unit with built-in gas fireplace, television, VCR and stereo, complete with a small collection of CDs and videotapes.

The only problem with this middle section of the space—if it could actually be called a problem—was that it offered no view. Any window larger than a dormer would have meant cutting into the roof, which must've been more than Zelda was willing to do. So she saw immediately why Zelda wanted her to create a faux-view with some sort of mural. Miranda's philosophy about murals was that they needed to be as realistic as possible so as to truly "fool the eye" as the French phrase indicated. Accordingly, she bent down to peer out one of the dormers, to see what the view *would* have been, had it been visible. *Rooftops, almost all of them red tile . . . tree tops . . . a glimpse of marina with matchstick masts . . . and a flat, shining strip of ocean with sails unfurled.*

She stood, stretched her back, and considered. The view

she'd examined only offered one perspective. Continuing to stand in the middle of the cozy room, she imagined instead that she stood on a flat rooftop with no walls at all. She took a moment to orient herself, recalling that—unlike most of the rest of California's coastline—this section ran East-to-West, rather than North-to-South. So toward what she thought of as east—according to the compass, actually north—she'd be seeing Santa Barbara's signature mountain range, probably tufted here and there with low-lying fog; to the "north and south," she'd see coastline trailing away; then "westward," there'd be that marina and ocean view. *So why not make the mural a three-sixty view?* Instantly, she fell in love with the idea. The upper, angled portions of wall she'd paint simply with pale blue sky and clouds. But the lower, upright portions—which came up about as high as five feet—she'd paint to match the imaginary view. *Mountain range to the east, ocean to the west, and serpentine coastline to north and south.*

While the idea was still so fresh in her mind, she began walking off the footage in the room, grappling with the proportions so her initial paper-sketches would be to scale. It was then she realized she hadn't yet explored the far end of the room, where she saw a wall with a door that must lead to the bedroom. Opening it, she stepped into the coziest space of all, with a built-in closet along the east wall, a queen-sized bed—also still factory-wrapped—and built-in end tables. The only window faced "south" which meant "east" on the compass, so it really was a morning room, where lemon-yellow light would angle in. But rather than continuing the landscape theme, she envisioned the sweet room as a garden. *I could paint a jasmine trellis on the angled ceiling to continue the courtyard theme . . . paint a window box with impatiens . . . a couple of gardenia bushes. Yes, and add a couple of large pots—with a couple of real ones too.*

It often worked this way for Miranda—a complete idea landing all at once, painting itself across the inner landscape of her mind. The trick now was to capture the *feeling* of it, if not every detail, before it fled, or got muddied by the intrusions of "good ideas" her helpful brain would try to offer. Already, she could feel them pressing at the edges of her consciousness: "too much green in this room will be overwhelming"; "the view-thing in the living room will get old"; "these ideas are so predictable." *Stop!* she ordered. And, dashing downstairs, she grabbed her sketchbook and began capturing the vision just as she'd first seen it, giving herself to the flow as it began to pour through her pencil and onto the white sheets of her pad.

17

Miranda Jones stepped into Andersen's Bakery and Restaurant on State Street, feeling she'd entered a café that might've been moved here from Solvang, the charming Danish town just up the Pass from Santa Barbara. With gleaming bakery cases filled with ornamented confections, white wooden chairs tucked under tables with pristine white cloths and bright buds in tiny vases, the room was as inviting as a grandmother's shiny kitchen. Mounted along a high beam above the long counter, a row of blue-and-white plates added a note of history. *Wonder if they're Delft? Or would the Danish take offense at having their Dutch dishes mis-identified? Mother would know.*

From the corner of her eye, she caught movement and saw someone was waving to her from a table by the window. She recognized Katy Sails immediately from the SOR brochure she'd read, a red-haired beauty with an earnest expression.

Walking to her table, Miranda extended her hand. "So good to meet you in person," Miranda began, and the two women sat down to talk.

"Likewise!" Katy dittoed. "I've been looking forward to this. I absolutely *love* your work!"

Not having expected the compliment, Miranda blinked, uttered a quiet thank you, then offered, "I've never painted otters at sea, though. I've seen them off the coast farther north, but never here, and never in the harbor."

Katy nodded. "From our phone conversations and emails, I know you've been doing some reading, so you have some of the basics."

"Basics meaning. . . ."

Katy paused for a moment, her gaze drifting toward the windows, as though she could see the ocean from where they sat. "Well, they're the smallest of the marine mammals. They live on the surface. I mean, all marine mammals have to come to the surface to breathe, but some of them spend almost as much time submerged; the otters, not as much. They live in bays, harbors, havens like Morro, Milford-Haven, Cambria, Monterey. The thing is, they eat, sleep, play, all in full view of humans."

"Right," Miranda nodded. "And I suppose that means they also see humans a lot."

"We have no idea what effect that has on them, or how much attention they actually pay to us, but yes, they can see us. They certainly interact with humans who spend time on or in coastal waters."

"And they make eye contact. That much I've seen for myself. I've seen their bright eyes tracking me when I walk along the boardwalk in Cambria."

A waitress stepped to their table. "Oh, we haven't looked yet," Katy said. "But I'd like some hot tea, for now."

"Hot tea here too," Miranda echoed. "And we promise we'll look at the menus soon."

"Okay, I'll get those teas and be back."

As the waitress walked away, Katy continued. "They're pretty amazing critters. Every time I think I know them pretty well, they surprise me."

"Surprise you . . . how?"

"Oh, you don't want to get me started!" Warming to her subject, Katy's face lit with animation. "They're smart—smarter than we think they are. Add to that the fact that they have articulating paws—a lot like hands in furry mittens . . . it's quite a combination. One of our workers at the Monterey Aquarium dropped his sunglasses in the tank. Sully retrieved them, then handed them back."

Not quite understanding the significance, Miranda sat waiting.

"Well, Sully is an otter."

"Oh!" Miranda exclaimed. "An otter went diving for the sunglasses, and returned them?"

"Absolutely."

"That's hilarious! And . . . daunting, too."

"Exactly," Katy said, beaming like a proud mama. "More typical behavior would be chasing after something in the water to play with it, maybe take it apart, definitely see how it tasted. But handing it back to its owner? That was a new one on all of us."

The waitress appeared again, and set two plates on their table, each holding a small metal pitcher of hot water and a mug. She returned a moment later with a wooden box, which she opened to reveal rows of tea bags, their delightful aroma lifting from the container.

"Earl Gray for me," Miranda chose.

"English Breakfast," said Katy.

While they dunked the tea bags, Miranda observed her new acquaintance. *Katy seems so excited about her work. She's not much younger than I am. That passion for the environment, and that red hair . . . easy to imagine how Samantha Hugo must have looked at that age.* Miranda reached into her bag to grab her notebook and a pen. "I just want to jot a few notes as we talk, if you don't mind. I never know when an idea will work its way into a painting."

"Of course. Let's see. Well, there are some things that wouldn't show in your painting, but you might want to know."

"Such as?"

"Nobody thinks about this much, but they live without fresh water, so they have powerful kidneys that get rid of salt."

"Right, never thought of that."

"Their eyes have tapetum, crystals that act like mirrors gathering all available light to their retinas. It's a special otter night vision."

"Wow, I sure hadn't read about that."

Katy tore open a packet of honey and drizzled its contents into her mug. "Of course, their pelts are a whole story unto themselves, one that almost caused their extinction."

"I've read quite a bit about that. No blubber to keep them warm, like other marine mammals. But the thickest, softest fur imaginable."

"Exactly. A human head has about 100,000 hairs. An otter has anywhere from 150,000 to a million per square inch."

"Incredible. And that's why they were almost hunted out of existence," Miranda added.

"Between 1742 and 1911, they were harvested commercially by Russian and American fur traders," Katy confirmed. "By the beginning of the twentieth century, there were only a few hundred animals left. In fact, by the 1930s, most people believed the California sea otter had completely vanished."

"Right," Miranda concurred, stirring her own tea. "And in 1938 that small group of otters was discovered living under the Bixby Bridge, right?"

"Exactly, in the mouth of Bixby Creek in Big Sur. And we think today's population of southern sea otters all come from that small group. Friends of the Sea Otter had a lot to do with protecting them."

Miranda nodded. "Margaret Owings. We *owe* her a lot. She's one of my heroes." Miranda took a sip of her Earl Gray. "And there's a lot more after that, the whole political situation surrounding otters. I'm not sure I understand it all."

Katy shook her head. "It's complicated. You'd probably have to talk to people on all sides of the issue to really get it. As for the animals themselves, I can give you all kinds of data—facts and figures. And I will. But once we've gone over some of the research materials, what I think you really need is time to observe them for yourself."

Miranda smiled, feeling her heart beat a little faster. "That's what I'm so excited about."

"Great," Katy remarked, "because I've arranged two different outings for you with a local outfitter and charter company."

"Oh, terrific."

"Yes, you'll like these guys. Dave and Doug. Well, you'll like Dave, for sure. Doug can be a little . . . salty."

"As long as he doesn't mind my intruding?" Miranda inquired.

"It's his job to have people intrude, so he'll just have to get over it." Katy smiled ruefully. "Okay, the first trip will be in a kayak with me. Dave has it all arranged. I'll be giving you a private tour along the coastline, so you'll work your way westward from where we are in the harbor."

"Sounds amazing."

"It is beautiful," Katy confirmed. "But you never know how much wildlife you'll see. That all depends upon their food supply, and at the moment the urchins here are still fairly plentiful. The urchins cling to the kelp holdfasts—where the blades attach to the bottom—and chew them, which is why we *want* the otters to eat the urchins, before they do too much damage to the kelp forest."

"Right, I've been reading about that," Miranda added. "And I also read a little about the commercial fishermen competing with the otters for the local urchin supply."

"Exactly. And that's where we run into some friction with Doug. He works on offshore oil rigs part of the year, and he's a commercial fisherman the rest of the time."

"Ouch. Seems like I won't agree with him on either count."

"Tell me about it," Katy agreed. "But really, he's a good guy, and incredibly knowledgeable. Those of us who work the waterfront find we all do better when we respect each other."

Miranda nodded. "Makes good sense."

"So tomorrow," Katy continued, "will be your kayak day. After I do my morning check of our otters, I'll meet you at D&D Charters and they'll have our equipment all ready to go. I've ordered us a lunch-bucket-to-go, and you won't need anything but a hat, sunblock, and your camera."

"Fantastic! But . . . I do have one more request. Could I peek at the otters in your facility before we take off?"

"Yup, no problem." Katy reached into a canvas bag she'd

hung over the back of her chair. "I brought you a bunch of paperwork, too. You'll need to sign a couple of forms. And you'll find some reading material. You do a little homework tonight, before we meet in the morning."

Miranda reached for the brochures and papers. "Excellent. I've been doing some research, but I knew you'd be a primary source. I might bring my sketchpad in the morning, if I can leave it in your office when we head out on the water?"

"Of course. I do have a nice surprise for you tomorrow. Several, actually. It'll be a fun day."

Miranda beamed at her new friend. "I am so grateful for all these arrangements!"

Katy smiled back. "Hey, we're the ones who are grateful. We're going to wind up with some Miranda Jones wildlife art!"

The two women laughed, and looked over as a waitress approached their table again. As Miranda glanced down at her menu, shafts of orange light from the setting sun strafed through the windows to paint bright bands across the table. Miranda knew the food would be good, but the conversation was already spectacular.

18

The next day, Dave Dax had been on his feet for two hours straight, handling the influx of customers on a busy morning. *Damn good thing I like people. Otherwise I'd be snarling by now.*

He glanced over at the middle-aged couple speaking a foreign language who'd been staring at the D&D Charters Menu of Services for about twenty minutes, still looking as baffled as they had when they first arrived. *I should go offer to help them . . . but now there's a line of folks who do seem to know what they want.*

Next in line was a fit-looking couple who turned out to be Will Marks and friend. He'd booked them by phone for their day-long kayak rental. After asking them a few questions, it seemed clear they knew their way around water sports, but weren't particularly familiar with this part of the coast. *She's from here, he's from Morro. What they need is a detailed map and a detailed conversation with me.*

"Okay, Will, good to meet you in person."

"Likewise." He smiled and offered a hand to shake.

"So, you're hoping to see some scenery and some wildlife, yes?"

"Exactly."

"Planning to pack a lunch?"

"Yes," the woman put in. "And maybe you can give us a recommendation about that, too."

"Absolutely. Right next door is the Sand Castle Café. Sandwiches, salads, drinks. And if you use this card—" Dave reached under his desk, brought out one of the coupon cards he'd had printed up specially—"they'll package it up for you and give you a discount."

"Perfect!" The woman smiled, and looked at her . . . boyfriend, it must be, as Dave didn't see a ring.

"Okay," Dave continued, "look over this map and give me a few minutes, okay? Then come back to the desk and I'll discuss some of your options with you."

"Sounds good," said Will.

Dave smiled, glanced again at the befuddled European couple across the small room, then looked up at his next customer. *Whoa! That's an intimidating guy if I ever saw one. He looks like he's about ready to bite my head off. That mole on his face doesn't help.* "How can I help you, sir?" he asked in his most affable tone.

"Need a boat."

"Okay. What kind?"

"Kayak."

The man said it as if this should be obvious, and Dave was a dunce for not having known. "Will this be a day rental? Or just a few hours?"

"I'll take it for the day," the man replied, pulling a wallet from his back pocket. When his hands appeared on the counter, they were calloused. *Must work the docks, or maybe construction. Looks like he could break a paddle in half.*

"Okay. I'll just need a credit card. We typically put a hold of—"

"No credit card," the man said in monosyllables. Then he produced a crisp hundred-dollar bill. "This work?"

"Uh . . . that should more than cover it, yes." Dave grabbed one of his pre-loaded clipboards. "Just fill out the information on this form, and when that's done, we'll go take a walk so you can pick out the kayak you'd like."

Without a word, the man grabbed the clipboard and headed for the one remaining chair against the wall, overpowering it as he sat awkwardly.

Takes all kinds, Dave thought to himself. *And that particular kind is not one I'd like to run into in an alley. Or out on the water, for that matter.*

Will and his friend stepped back to the counter. "We think we know where we'd like to go," Will said. "And Francine had a couple of questions, too."

"No problem. Let's go outside, look at the boats, and we'll go over the map."

As Dave led his two customers down the dock to review their kayak options, give them their paddles and life vests, he couldn't help but smile at the cheerful expressions on their faces. *Well, at least two people are gonna have fun on the water today. Thank goodness for small favors.*

19

Ezmeralda Worthington gave the knitting one more try, then cast the mangled mass of stitches to the far end of her sofa. She regarded the disreputable bundle of yarn with disgust.

"Trouble with your knitting, dear?" her husband asked.

Finding his customary patience a further irritant, Ezmeralda sighed, struggled to push herself up from the cushions, and headed for the kitchen.

"I'll have some tea, too, Dear. Then we can discuss our next trip."

Her answer was to bang two cups onto two saucers, fill the teakettle, then bang it onto a burner.

All he does is sit there all day, reading one thing after another. Can't he find something to do? It'd been like this ever since he retired from his job in maintenance at Cal Poly. He used to be so active with his projects at the school. Now he was constantly underfoot. How was a person supposed to stand it?

She watched the teakettle, waiting impatiently for it to boil.

Cedric Worthington—well hidden behind his newspaper just in case his wife should peer around the kitchen wall—shook his head and smiled. *Thank goodness her bark has always been worse than her bite.*

A few minutes later she reappeared, teacups rattling on the tray she carried to the small table that overlooked the valley. He joined her, gazing fondly at the view. "Look, Dear, it's your favorite color. The hillsides are all bright green."

"Lime green. I know. But I like wearing the color, not looking at it."

"And I like looking at you when you wear it," he said amiably.

His wife turned away from the window to squint at him. "Speaking of looking at things, that's all you seem to do these days. I mean, while you worked, I had my book club, my girlfriends, my shopping. But now that you're *home* all the time, I have to take care of you all the time."

"You know I can fend for myself when I need to, Dear. I think it'd be terrific if you still went out with your friends."

"You? In the kitchen? You couldn't boil an egg or make a tuna sandwich."

"I can make a tuna sandwich. Not nearly as well as you can, of course."

Ezme huffed.

Cedric took another sip of his tea. "I think the cure is for us to plan our next trip."

After a momentary silence, she nodded her head slightly. "I agree. It'd do us good to get out of here."

"Excellent. How would you like to go to Santa Barbara?"

Her eyes grew wide with shock. "Really? We can afford to go there?"

"Well, I found a Best Western just down the highway in Carpenteria for our lodging. But by day we can wander the streets, and in the evenings we can find nice places to eat. And we can do a little sight-seeing too."

Now her eyes crinkled. "You've got it all planned already, don't you?"

"I do. And we leave tomorrow."

"Trust you to give a girl *no* time to plan! I better go and pack!"

Leaving her tea untouched and now too cold to drink, she pushed back from the table and headed for their bedroom.

Cedric took another sip of his own tea, smug satisfaction settling over him. His wife had never been an easy woman. But if he'd wanted someone easy. . . . *It was all worthwhile to see her smile.*

20

Miranda Jones had followed the map given to her by Katy Sails, and now stood at the door of the SOR Marine Enclosure.

The structure resembled a warehouse, and she pressed open an industrial door, then blinked as her eyes adjusted to the relative dark inside. The tang of a briny odor hung in the air, and she walked toward an interior door. But what startled her was the sound of a baby crying. *Maybe one of the staff brought her child to work?*

Miranda knocked gently on the door, which was opened immediately by an employee.

"Miranda?" Katy called from within.

"Yes."

"Just in time!" she enthused. "Come in. We're just feeding Lulu."

Now she heard the sound again—but this time it was more

of a squeal. She stepped toward the waist-high tub to see a sweet furry creature that trembled in Katy's cradling hands. "Oooh!" she sang, "it's a baby! Oh, aren't you beautiful?" she cooed. "Aren't you adorable?" Tears began to prick at her eyes as she gazed at the little creature.

"Pretty cute, eh?" Katy said. "Want to hold her?"

Miranda inhaled sharply. "Could I?"

Katy nodded to her assistant, who handed Miranda a pair of special gloves. Once they were on, Katy said, "Step right up to the tub, now hold her with both hands, as you would a new-born human."

Miranda complied, breathlessly accepting the warm vibrating weight of the pup. "Yes, you are just precious, aren't you?" Unable to take her eyes off Lulu, Miranda murmured, "She does look like a baby in an otter suit. Almost sounds like one, too.

"She's trembling. Is she cold?"

"Oh, no," Katy reassured her. "With that fur coat, she actually gets too warm, unless she spends time in the cold water. We want to encourage her to regulate her own temperature by deciding when to climb in and out. But for now, it's all new."

"Yes," Miranda said softly. "It's all new!"

"If you gently lower her," Katy suggested, "you can hold her there for a few seconds while she gets used to the water."

The moment her fur touched the liquid, Lulu began vocalizing so loudly, Miranda was afraid she might be hurting her.

"It's okay," Katy reassured her.

"Now she sounds like a squeezy toy. A loud one!"

"Okay, that's enough for now." Katy accepted Lulu from Miranda, and the little otter was placed on her table where she was rubbed dry with a towel, a process Lulu seemed to relish.

21

urt Ostwald looked over the printed form on the clip-board and scowled. No way would he be able to fill in all this information—at least, not honestly. And coming up with a fake address wasn't easy without doing a little home-work—something he couldn't do away from his computer.

Have to wing it, he thought. *No big deal.*

By the time he'd handed over the made-up information, chosen his kayak, heard the spiel about safety, strapped on his life vest and started paddling out of the harbor, he was nearly out of patience entirely. Patience for people, that is, he rec-ognized. And as his strong shoulders and arms powered him through the water, he could feel himself begin to relax into the motion, and even smile to himself.

Stearn's Wharf slid past him, and he took care navigating through sailboat traffic as he made his way west along the south-facing coastline. For a while, he saw how close he still was to civilization. Campus Point and Isla Vista loomed, the conclave for privileged brats who attended UC Santa Barbara on their parents' money, and partied so hard he wondered whether they actually came away with educations.

The bird sanctuary at the UCSB Lagoon seemed to entice him into its calm waters, but there'd be nothing to see there but a bunch of water birds. *Waste of time, waste of space. They should reclaim the land, build something locals can actually use.* Burt had no time for tree huggers—or kelp huggers, he supposed he should call them here, where ridiculous arguments about environmental issues got too much coverage in the local press.

"Save the Otters!" proclaimed one headline. "Fishing Industry Jobs at Risk!" announced a competing article.

These otters might be cute, but they were just big water rats, as far as he was concerned. They ripped abalone right out from under the local fishermen, made themselves a nuisance to boaters, and had even been known to attack people. *The varmints should be shot. Too bad the authorities would be all over anyone who did. Then again, how would they ever know?*

Burt refocused on the coastline that continued to slide past, aware that he was having to paddle harder. *Heard there were strong currents here. I've got the arms for it.*

There was no particular reason Burt had decided on today's excursion, except that he considered this to be part of his homework. His primary employer was a shipping magnate. This being the case, it made sense to keep up with his ocean skills. *Never know when he'll want me handling something aboard a ship, in or out of port.* The required skill sets fell into two categories: down in or close to the water itself, and aboard one of his boss's immense ships. When one of the tankers was

in San Luis Bay adjacent to Morro, he always took time to polish a skill or two. But today was all about the hand-to-hand
combat with the ocean, its currents, its creatures, and its secrets. For these he had to keep his mastery of diving, paddling,
and sailing, and these were better practiced not in the calm
waters of a huge haven, but in this stretch of coastal ocean that
he knew would grow increasingly agitated as he approached
Point Conception.

It was here that two of California's most powerful currents
clashed, and where some of the state's worst maritime disas-
ters had famously occurred. *I'm not going as far as the point,
not in this dinky boat. I'll have to feel out the westbound current,
turn around when it gets too strong. Nothing I can't handle, so
far.*

Burt used his powerful triceps to lift his paddle, then dig
into the toughened waters that streamed toward Gaviota,
keeping an eye open for a likely spot to pull to shore and take a
lunch break. After all, he'd need to keep up his strength.

22

Miranda Jones followed Katy as they stepped into their rented kayak, taking the aft seat as requested. It'd been an hour since they'd left the otter facility, after which they'd stopped at D&D Charters, gathered their equipment, and carried it to the load-in location. Now—wearing life jackets, hats, rubber shoes, and sun screen—they were ready to push off from the narrow, shallow beach used by divers and kayakers.

"If you drop your paddle, don't worry," Katy said. "It floats. And if we capsize, don't worry about that, either. Everything is watertight and designed to float—even the cooler with our lunch. We just climb back aboard."

Miranda thought about her camera, glad she'd sealed it in a zip-lock bag inside her "waterproof" pack. "Okay. And if we get into a high sea?"

"Well, we won't today, but if there's a big wave, I'll head into it. Okay, here we go."

As they began paddling across the harbor, Miranda found herself feeling as small as an otter amongst the towering boats lashed to their moorings. In fact, Katy accentuated the sensation by guiding them between the pontoons of a huge catamaran, and they glided easily under its main deck to come out the other side, where they had to pay close attention to sailboat cross-traffic.

They passed an authoritative-looking pelican presiding over a dock, and a large sea star hugging tightly to the piling of a pier. They paddled past a buoy where harbor seals lollygagged, scratching, murmuring as if to say, "Move over, it's time for my nap."

Soon the sailboats were more spread out across the water in front of them, and when Miranda looked behind, the coastline with its mountain silhouette appeared as a landscape-seascape image that imprinted itself on her memory. *I'll be painting that for sure. Most people never see the coast from this vantage. It'll deserve a large canvas.*

Her paddle lifted in rhythm with Katy's as their craft gathered speed. "Look!" Miranda shouted, and Katy turned her head to nod and smile. Off their port side, a small pod of dolphins wheeled in the shallow waves, their dorsal fins gleaming in the sunlight.

"Oh, they're just spectacular!"

Katy laughed, evidently sharing in the joy of the exuberant creatures. Then, she turned again and resumed paddling, adjusting their course to parallel the coastline heading west. Miranda kept pace, noting the waves were small here, the water relatively quiet.

Even so, the steady exertion took its toll on muscles, and the sun beating through her hat caused some heat-fatigue.

After what seemed like another hour of paddling, Katy said over her shoulder, "We should pull to shore for a lunch break. There's a Reserve at Coal Oil Point."

"Okay!" Miranda agreed, and they made for shore.

The coastal strand of the Coal Oil Point Natural Reserve lay soft and quiet in the early afternoon haze, though there was a chill in the air. The apparently undisturbed dunes supported vegetation, making the terrain a tapestry of sand and plants bordered by blue-gray mountains.

Miranda helped Katy pull the kayak up onto the sand, and they began hauling grass mats and their small cooler. When they'd unrolled the mats, they sat and opened the cooler, taking out plastic-wrapped sandwiches and relatively cold bottles of water.

Biting into an avocado-and-tomato on whole wheat, Miranda realized she was hungrier than she'd thought.

"We'll probably see otters a little bit east of here," Katy commented between bites.

"So we're heading back?" Miranda answered.

"On the way here, we stayed farther out, but as we head back, we'll hug the shore between here and Campus Point. One of the larger kelp beds grows between the two points, so the otters love it."

"Sounds great. We must be near the University."

"Yup. Isla Vista is U.C. Santa Barbara student housing, and the university lagoon is another wildlife sanctuary."

Katy took another bite of her sandwich and chewed for

a moment. "The otters are almost always eating. They have to consume up to twenty-five percent of their body weight every day to survive, so they're either eating or looking for food about three times a day. And they eat primarily benthic invertebrates."

"What kind?" Miranda asked.

"Benthic—meaning bottom-dwelling. Urchins are their favorites. And they love abalone. But they also eat crabs, octopus, rock oysters, barnacles, sea cucumbers, even some bottom fish. All told, they have about 160 items in their diet. But they have their favorites. There are even food preferences in specific family groups. We think this is an adaptive technique that allows different groups to fish together without interfering with each other."

"I've seen them cracking open their food on their chests, floating on their backs."

"Right," Katy confirmed, "when they float on their backs, they can use their paws. You know, they're the only tool-users in the ocean."

"Like using a rock to break open an abalone?"

"Right, but they'll find tools, too, like an old can found on the ocean floor. Or they might steal something left on a dock."

"Clever little dickens."

"You know it!"

"So, how do they carry it all—their food, tools—and get it all back to the surface?"

"That's what their pockets are for."

Miranda nearly choked on a sip from her water bottle. "Pockets?"

"Well, they have loose, flexible skin, and they make pockets between their chest and arms when they need to store extra food or tools. That's how they carry so much back to the surface," Katy explained.

"Amazing. You know, because I've only seen them on the surface of the water," Miranda reflected, "I realize I've only seen about half, or maybe a third, of who they are, how they behave, what they actually do."

"Yeah," Katy nodded and rolled up the plastic wrap that'd held her sandwich, careful to stow it back in the cooler. "The way I planned your outings, today is for surface observation. Then day after tomorrow, when we head out to Anacapa, you can snorkel and get that underwater glimpse you want."

"Perfect!" Miranda exclaimed. "I really appreciate all the thoughtful arrangements."

"My pleasure. The more you know and can visualize the otters, I figure the better job you'll do with our mural."

"Yes, it's the only way. Best thing about my job—how much I learn along the way. You know, I just thought of otters as cute. And they're so much more," Miranda observed.

"They're cute and cuddly when they're grooming and feeding their young. But when you see how determined they can be to get at their food . . . some of the fishermen describe them as vicious."

"Really? I can't picture that."

"If they have to, they'll use a rock as a sledgehammer. If they're trying to free a hard-to-move mollusk, like an abalone, it might take several dives and multiple bashings."

Miranda raised her eyebrows. "Determined is right. How long can they stay down?"

"They can stay submerged for four or five minutes. When they're diving on deeper areas, it can take up to ninety seconds to reach the bottom."

Miranda reached into the cooler for the two apples that'd been packed with their lunch. "Want one?" When Katy nodded, she shook some of the ice-melt that dripped from the cool fruit, handed one apple to her, and bit into the other. After a moment she said, "It was amazing to hold little Lulu. I always wondered how otters might respond to human touch."

Katy munched, then said, "Pups like her are so special . . . so vulnerable. She was probably only a day old when we found her. Most likely she didn't get enough of natural antibodies from her mother's milk, so she needed constant care at first—feeding and grooming." Katy's gaze drifted out across the water. "She's number 299, you know?"

"You give each rescued otter a number?"

"We do—we number them chronologically, so she's the 299th since the program began in 1984."

"That's wonderful," Miranda said, "and terrible."

"That about sums it up."

"How do . . . why do the pups get abandoned?"

Katy sighed. "Most likely because their mothers get killed—orcas or sharks prey on them. Or sometimes the mother might be injured, too much so to care for the pup. And by the time she recovers, the little one is gone. If it's lucky, we find it in time and give it a home."

"But these rescue pups . . . can they go back to the wild?" Miranda wanted to know.

"Sometimes. If we have one, we pair a surrogate mom in captivity with the rescued pup, and if that works—if they learn the skills they'll need to survive—they do fine. They even go on to become mothers themselves, giving birth and tending their pups in the wild."

"How many get to return to the wild?"

"A lot—we tag them, and quite often we can then continue to track them for at least a couple of years. Of course, sometimes . . . we don't have a surrogate mother and then, well. . . ."

Miranda watched as Katy's sentence trailed off, as her eyes went dull. "You're doing beautiful work. You're doing the work you otter."

Katy guffawed.

Good. The little joke worked, snapped her out of her sad moment.

"As you can imagine, I've never heard *that* one before!"

"No, of course not," Miranda agreed.

"Ready to head out?" Katy asked. But Miranda was already carrying the cooler back to the kayak.

The moment they began paddling away from the beach, Miranda felt a tightness in the back of her arms, and knew her muscles would be talking to her later. Looking out to sea, she noticed a man paddling a bright yellow single kayak westward, perpendicular to their trajectory, but much too far away to cross their path. *Wow, he's moving fast. Powerful strokes. I could never keep up with him. Looks like he's on a mission.*

Katy turned her head to talk over her shoulder. "Listen, we talked about physical contact with the otters in captivity. But don't ever try for contact in the wild, okay?"

"Would it scare them?" Miranda asked.

"A wild otter will respond aggressively to touch. It'll try to bite you."

"Okay, good to know!"

"At the Center, we deal with wild ones who are very sick and can't care for their coats on their own. We have to groom them. Yikes! Some of them just hate that."

"Got it." Miranda figured a close encounter with a wild otter unlikely, but then again . . . she'd read they could be playful. *I'll just have to keep my hands to myself.*

They paddled eastward and spotted another kayak in the distance, its color bright orange, like their own. A man with dark hair sat aft, a woman sat forward, a hat concealing the color of her hair. Maybe they rented from D&D Charters, too. They seem to be heading in our direction, so they must be interested in local wildlife.

Just then, Katy spotted a pair of otters. "Check it out!" she called. "Eleven o'clock!"

Miranda turned her head slightly to the left, and there they were, a mother swimming backwards, her pup on her abdomen, her flippers paddling so efficiently she barely rippled the water.

Katy slowed her paddling, guiding their kayak to follow the otter mom, whose trail led toward a group of otters. "That'll be her home group," she explained. "They're rafting, taking turns diving for food and grooming their pups."

"Industrious!" Miranda said, hauling her camera out of her pack. To keep her trusty 35mm Nikon N90 safe, she'd brought its waterproof sleeve that protected the delicate controls on the body of the device. The lens itself was vulnerable to spray, so she'd do her best to be careful with it.

As they watched, quiet as their kayak drifted closer to the group, they saw two adolescents rotating like a furry Ferris wheel. Then they watched an adult use both her paws to massage her cheeks, as though her jaw muscles were exhausted by too much chewing.

"A cub can float away," Katy said quietly, "so the mom wraps it in kelp."

"Clever," Miranda commented, clicking the shutter.

Lowering her camera for a moment, she looked around to be sure not to include the other kayakers in her shot, but they'd apparently paddled elsewhere.

Katy added, "It can float away, but it can't drown, because there's too much air in its fur. It can't dive. It'd be like trying to submerge wearing a life jacket."

Miranda watched as one of the moms held her furry bundle on her tummy, licking the pup's pelt, keeping it well groomed.

"If she didn't do that—groom her pup and herself—the pelt would collect oils and debris that could prevent it trapping air efficiently. Then the animals risk getting cold—so cold they could die. So the grooming isn't optional."

During every wildlife photo shoot, Miranda experienced a moment when she knew—knew she'd captured something about the animal that would wind up on her canvas. She realized, suddenly, that it often had to do with eye contact. She flashed back to that moment with Lia the Cheetah in San Diego's Wild Animal Park, when the cat had stared right at her.

She'd been watching and waiting for it here, floating offshore amongst this peaceful, busy group of otters who seemed unperturbed at their presence, even generous in their embrace. *This might be it.* Click. *She's looking right at me.* Click. *But not the pup. It's looking at her.*

Miranda waited, camera poised, in case the pup's head came around in her direction, but now the mom moved on to her next task, wrapping the baby in a band of kelp and diving beneath the gentle waves. *That wasn't quite it. But I might get a nice shot of the mom feeding the little one in a few minutes.*

Sure enough, she did get to watch the feeding ritual, capturing several more images. When mom appeared, she brought a crunchy treat, chomped on the shell, then used her paws to tear out a piece of urchin and feed the mash to her offspring.

"That's quite a system they have," Miranda said. "This is how it's supposed to be in the wild."

"Oh, look. See that flash of bright color on the mom's flipper?"

Miranda used her camera lens to zoom in where Katy pointed. "Got it, yeah."

"Okay, that's one of our tags. That means we released her back into the wild at some point. And now she's a mom, raising a pup of her own."

Miranda could see how proud this made Katy, as if she were a mother herself. "That is so fantastic!" After snapping one or two more photos, she stowed her camera back in its double-protection. "So you do sometimes see them again."

"Quite often. We can't always recognize them. Some otters will chew their own tags off almost immediately, others leave them alone entirely, some have their tags chewed off by other otters."

Miranda chuckled at the funny image.

"On the other hand," Katy continued, "we have some otters out there who've had tags for ten years and the only thing that makes it difficult to identify them is that the color of the tag sometimes fades or changes."

"And that's the only way for humans to tell one from another?"

"No, some have distinguishing marks," Katy explained. "Let's see if I can find one." She lifted a small set of binoculars she'd placed around her neck and peered at the raft of otters. "Okay, yes, there's one." Pulling the binocular strap over her head, she handed them to Miranda, then pointed. "See that mom that has the pup facing backwards on her belly?"

Miranda looked carefully until she spotted the pair. "Yup."

"Okay, see the white slash across the mom's nose?"

"I do!"

"Females receive those scars during mating. Once they heal, she wears her own little tattoo. We pretty much always recognize those, so we can continue to observe them with some regularity."

"Aha. That's something I'll want to include in my painting." Miranda handed the binoculars back to Katy. "You realize that after this trip, I won't be able to resist doing an otter painting in addition to the mural."

Katy smiled. "It'll be a beauty, I have no doubt."

"So, um, how do you find them in the first place? I mean you don't come out here and paddle for miles just in case you recognize one of your otters, right?"

Katy grinned. "Now I'll have to tell you *another* one of our secrets."

Miranda laughed.

"All the pups are released with a radio transmitter which emits a signal that can be picked up as long as we have a receiver. This is how our trackers find known otters. The transmitter battery only lasts about two years, though, so unless we recapture them and replace the transmitter—which sometimes we do—the only definitive way to identify them after a few years is by flipper tags."

"You and your team are so devoted," Miranda said, feeling awed at their commitment.

Katy said nothing in reply, and began to paddle.

So unselfish, Miranda thought. *All the help they give the mothers and the pups ... and mostly anonymously.* She reflected on Katy's work as they began to paddle back to Santa Barbara.

The two women paddled smoothly back into the harbor. Miranda was preoccupied, processing everything she'd seen during the day when Katy drew her attention to the stern of one of the boats docked in a slip.

"See that?" Katy pointed. "That's adaptive behavior."

"Sorry, what in particular?" Miranda asked.

"There's a mom who's used to living among humans. She's gotten very comfortable, swimming among the boats, even climbing up on them."

Sure enough, Miranda watched as an otter mom hefted herself onto the swim-shelf of the boat, then pulled her pup up after her. Then, leaving her pup safe, the mom slipped back into the water.

"The mom's gonna dive for food. Normally, she'd wrap the pup in kelp, but she's found an easier way," Katy explained.

"She's found a play pen," Miranda commented.

"And the interesting thing is, the mom will teach all the behaviors she herself knows. Which means it's likely her pup will do the same if it becomes a mom."

Katy guided their kayak out of traffic toward the boat, careful not to get too close. When the mom surfaced again, she held a treasure in one paw, a rock in the other. The women heard the "tap tap" of the rock on the shell, and soon the mom was offering the contents, depositing the tasty treat into the tiny paws of her offspring.

He consumed the food. "Myah!" he complained, making it very clear he wanted more. "Wah wah wah."

She disappeared again, and brought back a gleaming shell, which she began to scrape. When she finally gave him his next bite, he worked hard to chew on it. Then he seemed to purr his contentment as it slid down his throat and into his tummy.

"That's an abalone," Katy said. "Tougher meat. That's why he chewed harder."

"Aha . . . not so hard when it's *uni*."

"Right, urchin is already soft," Katy concurred.

As if she knew she was being observed, the otter mom turned to stare at the humans.

Darn, Miranda thought, *my camera's packed!*

But then she realized the otter wasn't staring at her, but at Katy.

"That *is* you," Katy said under her breath.

"You know her?"

"She's one of ours. And she's a mom now herself."

Miranda sat in wonder. "It's as if . . . she recognized you."

"I think she does. They do have good memories," Katy said simply.

Miranda stared at Katy, then back at the mother, until the otter returned her attention to the pup.

And who's the mother? Miranda wondered. *It's not all about biology. It's about caring, nurturing, and . . . remembering.*

Tired, delighted—and awed—Miranda helped paddle the kayak back to the small beach where their day's adventure had begun.

23

Will Marks slowed his paddling as he said, "There they are, a group of otters. Want to watch them for a few minutes?"

"Absolutely," Francine agreed.

Will had been keeping an eye on their location, checking landmarks along the shore so as not to get lost or travel too far out. He'd noticed two women in a kayak that matched their own, apparently observing some sort of wildlife. Deciding it'd be a good idea to follow suit, he'd suggested they head for the kelp beds.

So far, their day together had gone well. *Better than well,* he thought. *Easy. Fun. Beautiful.* That last observation referred to the scenery both outside and inside their kayak. He was glad he'd taken the aft seat, as it'd given him a chance to watch her form and function. *Turns out she wasn't kidding about being athletic, and liking the water.*

As they'd paddled together, they'd fallen into an easy rhythm. Conversation was difficult, since it required the fore paddler to crane her neck, and in any case the breezes tended to carry words away. So he'd used the susurrus of the wind and waves to contemplate this woman whose company he enjoyed. It'd been a good plan, he decided, to choose an activity that took them both out of their comfort zone. Usually so impeccably groomed with sleek, shiny golden-brown hair that scooped just under her chin, now her strands poked out from under her hat in cute disarray. Her ramrod straight posture had relaxed and she seemed comfortable revealing this casual side of herself.

"Looks like they're sort of tangled in the kelp," she observed, holding her paddle across her lap.

"From the little I've read, they like the kelp."

Something flipped close by. "Oh!" Francine let out an exclamation. "Are they trying to get under the kayak?"

"Uh, well, I'm not sure. Not carrying any unwrapped food, are you?"

"No, they said not to," Francine confirmed. "Maybe they're playing."

"I've heard they like that, too."

Francine glanced toward the coastline. "We're pretty close to shore, here. I thought we'd have to be farther out to see them."

"You know, they're bottom feeders, and they have to dive for their food," Will commented.

"Oh, right, so they don't go into very deep water," Francine said. Just then, a face popped out of the water and Francine let out a peal of laughter. "Where did you come from?" she asked the critter. "I don't have anything for you, sorry."

Will found himself laughing too, not only at the close encounter, but at Francine's evident ease and lack of fear. *I think I could take her anywhere.*

"Oh, look! Two of them are touching noses! Just adorable."

"You call it adorable, I call it something more," Will commented.

"Romance on the high seas?"

"And elsewhere," he said.

She turned her head to look at him, and her brown eyes danced with mischief.

He held her gaze for a long, smoldering minute. "Should we head back?"

"I think we better. I wouldn't want to capsize."

"Heaven forbid," he said, beginning to paddle harder than he had all day.

24

Burt Ostwald continued to power westward along the coastline, reveling in his own strength and in the solitude.

Though he knew his temporary construction job in Milford-Haven was a good—and necessary—cover, today brought home the realization that "making nice" with phony colleagues in a phony job was far more exhausting than the job itself. Today's activity suited him perfectly: physically challenging, mentally easy.

He glanced behind him. A pair of women in a kayak wearing stupid-looking hats were dawdling off Isla Vista. *Probably tourists looking at the "cute critters" in the water.* They started to make for shore, maybe to explore the bird sanctuary, or to take a lunch break. He turned away immediately, lest they feel his gaze.

And that decided him. He'd skip having his own lunch on

a beach somewhere. What was the point? He wanted to avoid contact with anyone, and the rental came with a packed lunch. Against the advice of the charter people, he'd also brought some fresh crab meat—a favorite delicacy he seldom enjoyed.

He glanced north where the Santa Barbara Shores County Park bordered the sand, then watched where Sandpiper golf club draped its absurdly green turf along the shore. Along the way he spotted the forced cheerfulness of umbrellas and awnings at a resort. How artificial it all looked, and how frivolous. Gradually the world of humans and their activities began to seem foreign as he moved farther from habitation.

Deciding he was hungry, he stowed his paddle and opened the small cooler that was supposed to contain his lunch. He unwrapped the sandwich. *Vegetarian. Figures.* He polished it off in a couple of quick, unsatisfying bites. He was tempted to toss the apple overboard. The energy it took to digest an apple pretty much used up the calories it offered, but food was food. Since that, and a bottle of water, exhausted the so-called "meal" he was glad he'd be able to augment with his own stash. But rather than gorge, he decided to resume his course and nibble along the way.

He drew open the zip-lock bag of succulent crab and placed it on his lap. He reached for a healthy chunk and filled his mouth with a huge, delicious bite. Still chewing, he poked his paddle back into the water. Almost immediately it caught in a strand of kelp. "Shit!" he said, pulling free and aiming farther from shore. "Damn kelp. It's a damn hazard," he muttered.

Something flapped at the edge of his kayak. Thinking it was another tendril of the slimy plant, he paddled more vehemently to free himself. But then, just past his bow, a *head* popped above the surface! "Get!" Burt yelled. "Get the hell away from here!"

The monstrously ugly whiskered head with its bulbous nose was attached to a slick body that moved like greased lightning through the water. It popped up again, this time on Burt's port side. He knew from the animal's size this was no adult, but an adolescent, with the teen-attitude to prove it. It lifted its upper body out of the water, trying to use its paws to gain purchase on the kayak, its short arms slip-sliding over the slick fiberglass surface.

Diabolically clever paws grabbed at whatever they could, ripping at the jacket lashed under Burt's legs. Burt used his paddle to poke at the beast, successfully shoving it away. But now it latched on, hanging off the long stick as if taking a free ride. Burt shook the paddle, rocking the kayak precariously until the otter dropped off, only to reappear by Burt's elbow. A furry arm darted out, claws extended, grabbing for the plastic bag of crab now lodged between Burt's legs.

"Fuck!" Burt screamed, as the creature swiped danger-ously close to his private parts.

Burt felt fear and revulsion course through his body and take a firm grip on his mind. *The deformed flippers with their toes running backwards . . . the beady eyes that fixated on him from the coarse-haired skull . . . the gleam of sharp teeth.*

Now he found himself in the grip of a terror so severe, he hardly recognized himself. *Like a monster-movie. No, like the worst nightmare. Haven't felt this since . . . since my demon step-father came at me.* It was all he could do not to leap from the kayak. *But that would do no good.*

He heard a flap in the water, saw the flash of the dark body.

It came again, desperate to get the crab. And this time Burt was ready for it. Holding the paddle like a bat, he thwacked at the otter and sent it careening overboard with a thud and a deep splash.

Burt sat in the kayak breathing heavily, eyes and ears tuned for another attack. But now, the water lay still, but for a lazy stipe of kelp that trailed past. Slowly, at first, and then more quickly, he paddled away.

25

The otter mom grabbed the scruff of her nearly-grown pup and pulled him farther into the kelp. Wrapping him in strands, she squealed at him, pleading for a response.

The pup's inert body floated and he gave no answer. He seemed to be in a sound sleep, though she sensed his hurt.

Hurt. Breathe. Breathe again.

An odor clung to his fur—crab, one of his favorites. Perhaps this was why he'd climbed aboard the craft, though she'd always discouraged him from making contact with humans.

The scent gave her an idea. Quickly, she dove for a treat, surfacing a few minutes later with a live crab. She crunched into it for him, placed a succulent morsel on his tummy. Still, he failed to respond.

She would keep him safe, tend to him, until he could fend for himself again.

Somewhere close, a danger lurked. She smelled human. *Sometimes safe. Sometimes not.* Where was he? Still close by? She blinked, but it was still too light for her night vision to help.

Sunset gleamed over the water, the shine bouncing.

Orange light, soon gone. Protect pup. Keep watch.

26

Miranda Jones had been so glad to see a tub in Zelda's guest suite that she'd stripped off her briny clothes, filled the porcelain with hot water and Epsom salts, then slid in to soak.

What a day . . . what an adventure! She watched the inside of her eyelids as a slide show of images scrolled. Lulu the tiny otter . . . the breathtaking profile of the mountains from the sea . . . the industrious otter group feeding, grooming, tending their young. Katy and her compassionate mission.

And now, here I am in this beautiful place. Zelda had chosen a bright pink paint for the bathroom walls. *I'd never choose it, but it does make me feel . . . like I'm in the pink!* She chuckled at the idea, noticing she was, in fact, turning pink in the heated water.

She loved both reasons for being in Santa Barbara—the otter mural, and the Zelda mural. *Similar . . . and different. Both a beautiful challenge. Zelda's would be enjoyed only by herself and her guests. The SOR mural would be seen by thousands.* Pondering further, she realized the goal of any mural was to transform the space where it stood, causing a wall to appear as something other than it was. And yet, a mural had to be more than illusion. It had to reveal an underlying reality.

For example, in the compact apartment upstairs, had it been physically possible to have the south-facing wall made of glass, and were there no buildings to obscure the view, a person in the room would see a panorama of the coastline. And soon, that's what they *would* see, because of the mural.

I love my job, she thought, beginning to drift into a watery dream. She bolted awake, wary of falling asleep in the tub. *Time to drag myself out.*

Miranda's stomach growled. It'd been several hours since that sandwich on the beach, and now that the sun had set, dinnertime had arrived. Dressed in some comfortable sweats, she padded to the kitchen to examine the food supplies Zelda's houseman had laid in. Fresh fruits . . . the makings for a salad or two . . . In the freezer, she found a container hand-labeled as "Farfalle with salmon." Her mouth started to water the moment she saw it, and she popped it in the microwave.

While it heated, she went to retrieve some reading material from her bag. Though in the future she'd likely stay in the small suite upstairs where she was doing the mural, during this trip she'd been invited to use the main floor guest room. Like everything else Zelda owned, the room revealed a sense of elegance and style. Antique French doors had been fashioned as headboards for the twin beds, and the walls were painted a daffodil yellow. *Another color I'd never have thought to use, but it's marvelous! Makes the room feel sunny, though it gets no direct light from the windows.*

In her backpack, she found the brochures she'd collected from Katy and from D&D Charters this morning. She also found the paperback book Kuyama had given her and knew this would be tonight's reading assignment.

For now, she pulled a bottle of sparkling water from the fridge, served the heated pasta on a plate, and sat at the kitchen table to eat and peruse the literature about otters and the Channel Islands.

When she'd washed the dishes and cleaned the kitchen, Miranda settled on the couch to read the paperback. Even from the introduction, a haunting sadness lifted from the pages, a tale of a woman whose language no one else understood, who'd been buried at the Santa Barbara Mission by a priest to whose church she did not belong, and whose ways she did not understand.

That much of the story was true. Much of it, however, was the imaginative interpretation of the marvelous author Scott O'Dell. The Island of the Blue Dolphins was the poetic name he'd given San Nicolas, the outermost in the string of Channel Islands, and, according to the brochures, the most desolate and storm-swept.

Piecing together every shred of history available, O'Dell had crafted a novel about the thriving colony of people who'd lived there, clever in hunting and fishing and in the crafts with which they created clothing, utensils, dwellings, and money and ornate jewelry made of shells. But a disaster befell them when Russians brought skilled Aleut sea otter hunters to the island waters. Greedy and dishonest, they'd murdered the chief rather than keep to the agreement they'd made to share the prized pelts.

Though the people recovered from this tragedy, months later white men's ships came to take the people away. To greater opportunities? Perhaps. But when all the people and their goods were aboard, one boy had been left behind. Sailing with the tide and anxious to avoid a storm, the captain would not return for him. So the girl—the protagonist of the story—flung herself overboard and swam for shore. The ships had promised to return for them . . . but they never did. And when her younger brother died, the girl was left to grow from child to woman all by herself.

For years, she watched the horizon. Yet ultimately, even the notion of returning ships became irrelevant, as she labored to fulfill the tasks once performed by an entire tribe. Yet she did it, found her way, befriended animals, read the winds, understood the seasons, found her way.

Once—only once—Aleuts returned to hunt, and with them came a girl her own age. Tentatively, furtively, they established a friendship even without a common language. They gestured, shared food and parting gifts.

Miranda thought back to her own childhood, so rich with companionship. With her sister she, too, had climbed hills and gazed out at the ocean. But rather than forage for food, they'd had a mother to pack lunches and to watch for their safe return.

They'd had friends and playrooms, treats and surprises, games and dolls, pets and projects—all thanks to their mother. All that privilege had come with responsibilities, expectations, and pressures. So much so, that Miranda could remember that when her mother called to her, she'd wait till the third call before answering. She hadn't wanted to interrupt her play, or to be scolded for something she'd done wrong—and there was always something.

So, she'd imagined a life with no parents. *No mother to argue with, no father to try to please. I've sometimes wished for exactly that.* A stab of guilt knifed into Miranda as she realized how devastating the loss would actually be. The girl in the story had lived it. She'd have done anything to hear her mother call, or listen to her father admonish. All she had was silence and solitude. *Could I have borne it so bravely? Could I even have survived?*

Karana. Miranda closed the book and whispered the fictional name of the brave woman who'd lived so fiercely on the hills and canyons of the jutting island. *Which parts are true? Everything in the novel seemed so real, I feel I know the character.*

How excited Karana had been to sit in the sunlight with the friend who visited her island so briefly. How kind she'd been to the dog whom she transformed from enemy to faithful companion. How long her prayers had gone unanswered, and how courageous and self-reliant had been her way.

I wish I could have been your friend and shared secrets with you on the windy cliffs. I hope I can find a way to honor your spirit.

Thinking of the long-lost girl, Miranda slipped into a dream of the Island of Blue Dolphins.

27

Will Marks rolled off Francine and waited as his hammering heart began to slow.

"Wow." Francine spoke the word on a gasp, still catching her breath. She glanced over at Will, then laughed.

"What?" he asked, a smile pulling at his lips.

"You don't have to look so smug," she complained.

"Oh, but I do."

She laughed again, then said, "Maybe we should go kayaking more often."

"Maybe so. Or we could blame it on the otters."

"Meaning?"

"There were a lot of babies out there. There must be a lot of hanky-panky."

She chuckled. "You're silly. They were awfully cute, though. So glad we got to see them."

"Same here," Will added. "The other thing those otters do all the time is eat. I'm starving."

"Oh, good, I thought you'd never ask."

"Ask what?"

"Whether I'd like to have dinner. The answer is yes, I would."

"Is that so?" he teased. "Well, who says I'm through with you?"

"Oh, I didn't say anything about being *through*. I will, however, require further sustenance before resuming any athletic activities."

He pondered that for a moment, then asked, "Pizza?"

"Perfect," she agreed.

Referring to the hotel's in-room list of local restaurants that offered delivery, he'd ordered two mediums: one with chicken and pineapple, one with shrimp and feta. While they waited, bundled in hotel robes, they watched a news story about corporate fraud, the reporter citing enough instances to support his claim that fraud was on the rise.

"I wonder how much really gets reported," Will remarked. "Like that Texaco thing."

"Not familiar," Francine said.

"Ten years ago. Texaco had a legal battle with Penzoil and was found owing ten-point-five billion. They declared bankruptcy, and later got taken over by Chevron."

"A giant saving a giant."

"At Clarke Shipping, we work with small indie oil companies. I just wonder, sometimes, how the big guys function." He hit the mute button during a commercial. "Ever think about corporate ethics?"

She'd been pulling a comb through her hair and halted at his question. "Just in case we wanted to choose a light little topic of discussion?"

"Yeah, sorry, I was just thinking about something at work. Probably not a big thing, but something I overheard. An employee was being asked to take care of some personal business for the boss."

Francine thought for a moment. "I imagine that can be tricky."

"Is there a point where you draw a line, refuse the assignment, threaten to quit your job?"

She was already shaking her head. "A situation would have to be dire for me to go that far. I figure it's hard enough to get a good job with benefits."

"True. But is there something that would really push your buttons?"

Her face became serious. "Aside from the sexual harassment and gender prejudice I already deal with?"

He saw that color had risen in her cheeks. "I didn't mean to—"

She put a hand up as if to stop him. "I love people, which is a damn good thing, given that I have to deal with the public every day that I work. Airline employees see it all, believe me."

"I try to imagine."

"And behind the scenes, pilots can be a problem, too. Mostly, I can handle whatever comes at me. But I expect fairness, integrity, a code of conduct from my employer."

He nodded. "Me too," he said. It was another point of agreement with a woman he both liked and respected.

They consumed both pizza pies in bed, using towels for a table-cloth, and drinking bottled water they'd found in the mini bar.

Steering clear of news, they scrolled through the channels till they found a new cable drama called *La Femme Nikita.*

"Killer body," Will said between bites.

"And she *is* a killer, too," Francine commented, licking her fingers.

"You better believe it," Will mumbled.

Francine squinted at him. "Maybe we'll change the channel."

"Oh, she has *nothing* on you, Queen of Kayaks."

Giggling, Francine said, "Okay, as long as you don't get any ideas."

He waggled his eyebrows. "I've got plenty of ideas. Had enough to eat?"

"Mm hmm," she said, swallowing.

"In that case, I have a suggestion about dessert."

28

The otter mom poked and prodded at her young one, as he lay heavy on her abdomen. Daylight had winked out when the sun dipped into the sea.

She vocalized at him, her mouth close to his ear. Her job was to feed and protect, find food and play, keep him safe, teach him the otter ways.

Suddenly, he woke.

She screamed at him, her pent fear demanding reassurance and sounding alarm.

But the pup, having found a food source, seemed now more determined than ever to have it. Leaping off his mother, he plunged back toward the human with tasty crab treats, his mother in desperate pursuit.

Burt Ostwald looked around to check his landmarks, and had to admit he'd made very little progress. This, however, was the better option, considering that the alternative scenario would have him swept along the coast, gripped by the southbound current at the Point. Adding to the problem, he'd be losing the last of the light in the next few minutes, and he didn't want to fight both the currents and the dark at the same time. He did, however, want to test his skills at navigating in dark water. He'd have to be close in to shore, where he'd need to listen for rocks and watch out for idiot boaters who'd stayed out too long and didn't have the experience to get ashore safely.

He heard it then—a scream bouncing its way across the water.

From shore? Is there a woman drowning? Is she being attacked?

He heard it again—closer now, yet no boat or craft approached.

He heard a squeal and saw a dark shape next to the kayak. *The damn pup—it's back!* It was too close, now, for Burt to wield his paddle effectively, but the critter wasn't so huge or heavy that he couldn't grab it. *I've got an empty pull-string bag . . . could stuff it in there, keep it from biting and scratching.*

Burt managed to stow his paddle without letting it slip overboard. Then, while the pup reached again for the crab meat, Burt grasped him by the scruff of his neck. "Gotcha!" he muttered, trying to use one hand to hold open his bag, while using the other to force the wriggling body into it.

Over the noise of the pup's continuous squeals, he thought he heard another lower-pitched squeal coming from across the water. *Shit, that could be the mom. At least she's a ways off.*

But she wasn't. Burt heard a slap on the water and turned his head just in time to see a set of vampire teeth bared as a huge head lunged out of the water, scaring him so badly he nearly flipped the kayak. The creature screamed again, the sound unearthly, plaintive, and menacing as anything he'd ever heard in his life.

Monster! Has to be the mother. Nothing worse than a pissed-off female.

He dropped the bag holding the pup, and heard himself shouting as he fended her off, poking with the paddle, afraid he'd lose it in the struggle. Burt saw her grab for the trapped pup, but only manage to snag a string.

She came at him from the other side, using her sharp claws to slice at his leg.

"Damn it!" he yelled. "Get away!" In the fading light, he could see his voice had momentarily startled her, its volume and deep tone, elements she seemed to be processing. But she came at him again, beady eyes focused, teeth bared, until she had him by the left arm.

Now *he* screamed, as her fangs pierced clothes and flesh. That's when he thought of the pellet gun. He had to reach one-handed into the pack under his legs. He felt for the zippered compartment where he'd placed the weapon and when he felt the cool metal, he grabbed it.

He shot the otter point blank in the head. At last, the vise-grip of the deadly teeth let go of his arm, and the creature slipped into the dark water. *Good riddance*, he thought.

Just before she sank from view, he noticed the drawstring of his bag slide off her arm, the pup beginning to emerge from the water-logged sack. *Too bad the pest didn't follow its mother to the bottom. Without her, it probably won't last long anyway.* His own pain then drew his attention away from the mournful mewing that accompanied the splashes of the bereft creature.

Burt knew he was bleeding, but had no idea how severe the bite was. Blood no longer oozed from the slice down his leg, and he still felt strong enough to paddle back to shore.

He couldn't be seen in this condition, however, so he thought it through quickly. He'd put in at the deserted beach he knew about between Gaviota and Refugio State Park. From there, he'd have to haul his gear, and the kayak, up the hill. He'd find a place to hide the kayak, walk to his motel, and return for the kayak before dawn so he could leave it at the rental place. *If it's not returned, they'll start looking for me . . . and my fictitious name will be suspect. Best not to give them any reason to suspect anything. Just a late return.*

He'd clean his wounds as best he could, then visit that quack he knew who could stitch him up, if necessary, and start him on a series of rabies shots. *This'll be a pain, in more ways than one. Other than that, Mrs. Lincoln. . . .*

But mishaps came with the territory. Tonight, he'd vanquished the foe, and would live to see another day. He paddled hard against the current, making for shore.

29

Miranda Jones peered out the windows of Zelda's kitchen, watching early morning light touch the tops of the mountains. Eager to get her day started, she stepped to the counter to use the Vitamix blender. She'd noticed the machine the night before and now she'd create what her mother would call "a concoction," taking advantage of how it could process whole fruit without leaving chunks or getting clogged.

Someday I'll be able to buy one of these for myself. Into the large canister she plopped a whole orange, peeled of course; a whole apple, cored but not peeled; a couple of scoops of the Shaklee protein powder she'd brought with her, and half a banana. Now the machine whirred and growled, pulverizing the contents until a fragrant orange-colored smoothie was ready to pour. *Perfect! Now I just need a cup of tea to take upstairs.*

She had the day all planned in her head: paint primer on

the walls; while it dried, finish her sketches on the huge pieces of newsprint she'd packed; pin the sketches to the wall to check for proportion and placement; then paint the mural.

Just as she was about to head upstairs, ideas began coming. But they were for the otter mural, she realized. *Makes sense, after spending the day with them yesterday.* After grabbing her sketchpad from the bedroom, she returned to the kitchen and sat at the table, quick pencil strokes capturing a rough outline of the exterior mural she'd do for SOR.

She'd turned the page sideways so she could work with a landscape aspect. About halfway up the page, she drew a horizontal line representing the surface of the water. Above it would be a mountainscape as seen from offshore. Below it, strands of kelp would stretch up from the sea floor, with all kinds of creatures depicted across the bottom of the image: urchins, sea stars, crabs, abalone—all the otters' favorite foods. Then, on the surface of the water, an otter and its pup would float. *Would they both be facing the viewer? Maybe. Not sure yet.* But the basic structure of the piece had presented itself clearly in three sections: above, on, and below the ocean surface. *Got it!* Smiling, she closed the sketchpad and climbed the stairs.

It took only an hour to finish the primer. Fortunately, Zelda's new furniture was already swathed in old sheets, or still wrapped in factory coverings. All she'd had to do was pull things a bit farther away from the walls, so she could slide herself along the floor as she gave the smoothly finished and taped sheetrock the initial coat it needed.

She made a quick trip down to the kitchen to fix herself a fresh cup of tea, then stepped out onto the small second-story balcony to ponder the view. Buildings of white-washed stucco formed geometric shapes, and red tile roofs, their patterns running like elaborate stitching in rectangles and squares, circles and wedges, spread out across the city. Palms poked upward into a pale blue sky, and lush ficus trees with their sculpted trunks and branches decorated the tapestry like fat pulls of rich green yarn. Orange and blue market umbrellas dotted patios and balconies. Carved mountains etched one horizon while blue water painted the other, and low-lying clouds drifted like tufts of cotton along the edge of the hills. Pale yellow and lemon sunlight gilded the east facing buildings.

From this height the ocean stretched like a vivid teal satin ribbon bisecting the view to her right. As the sharp water line traveled east—to her left—the ribbon widened to a strip of grosgrain that folded back on itself as water gave way to mountains. To make the ocean and the coastline more visible in her mural, she'd need to "cheat" the altitude of her vantage point, pretending she stood atop a twenty-story structure. From there, the band of blue water would appear five times wider, and the arc of the coastline would curve out toward Point Conception. *That way I can even include the lighthouse as a tiny structure at the far end of the image.*

The specifics of Zelda's mural now came at her so fast, Miranda rushed inside to begin her sketches. Soon, she knew, the complex image would start to paint itself in her head.

30

Everyone spoke at once, practically shouting to be heard.

   ". . . found early this morning. . . ."

   "Necropsy. . . ."

"Exactly where?"

"Horrible!"

"Terrifying."

"Shooter must still be. . . ."

"Law enforcement. . . ."

A shrill whistle pierced the air, cutting off the cacophony of noise, which then echoed for a moment through the warehouse that held the SOR otter tanks.

"Thank you," a man everyone else knew only by job description said to the circle of people sitting on folding chairs. "I'm Theo Renwick, Special Agent with U.S. Fish and Wildlife Service," he said. "I appreciate all of you interrupting your morning and coming on such short notice. Usually we keep an investigation under wraps but, as you know, word got out fast about this incident. I thought it'd be helpful if all of you attended this meeting."

The others in the room were silent for now, the mood somber.

"Special thanks to you, Katy, for letting us meet here at Sea Otter Rescue."

"Glad to help," Katy replied, nodding from her chair. "I apologize for using this space. I thought it'd be more private and certainly larger than our office on the Wharf."

"Okay," Theo continued. "As you all know, we've had a fatality. The only otter deaths we don't mind dealing with are those by natural causes."

Katy put in, "It's bad enough when we hear about a shark attack and lose one—especially one that's been rescued and released. But this—" She looked away, pressed her lips together.

Theo said, "This is a bad outcome for all of us, for all our agencies, for tourists, for other wildlife. Because it indicates there's a killer in our area."

A murmur rumbled through the room.

To get things back on track Theo suggested, "How about if each of you introduce yourself, then explain your connection to this case. Once we do that, we can start to structure a response. You know it won't be long before the press will be all over this story, and we should try to be on the same page."

Katy fell silent and looked to her left, where Pete sat next to her.

"Pete Simms, Geological Survey, USGS. I found her early this morning," he said, his voice grave. "Usually we wouldn't necessarily find an otter so soon after death, but I happened to be searching for a tagged otter after a report of several in the area. I noticed a dark shape on the beach and confirmed it was an otter through my scope. When I got down to the beach, found her and gave her a cursory exam, it seemed to me she'd been shot. So I brought her in."

"What time was this?" a man in a Sheriff's Department uniform asked as he started taking notes.

"Just after 0600," Pete replied.

"I'm Leo Garza, Warden, California Department of Fish and Game. So yeah, Pete reported it to us. And since he got her to the lab so quickly—and since this is an illegal human-caused killing of a federally listed species, we reported it to Special Agent Theo."

"Deputy Del Johnson," said the man who'd already started taking notes. "I'm with SPO—Special Projects—for SLO County. Other business had brought me to Santa Barbara, and dispatch contacted me, knowing I was already here." Del looked at Theo. "Appreciate being included, and I realize it's a courtesy to bring me in peripherally," he said. "We may have a related case, which is why I made the request. Working fast, and working together, will make it much more likely we can solve your case, and maybe mine."

Doug raised a hand. "Doug Haliwell with D&D Charters, but also with Commercial Divers. Pete, you said Gaviota. Exactly where did you find the otter?"

"Vista Point," Pete said, "washed ashore."

"Washed . . . or pulled herself there?" Doug wondered.

Pete thought for a moment. "No evidence of a crawling trail on the sand. She was in the high tide wrack. So it appears to me, at least, that she drifted in dead with the tide."

The Deputy made more notes while comments erupted around the room.

"Please!" Theo repeated. "Let's speak in turn!"

When the room quieted, Katy spoke up. "I was out yesterday, kayaking along the coast. I had a painter with me—Miranda Jones—we hired her to do a mural for us. We didn't get as far west as Gaviota, but we did see two other kayaks. One was yellow so it was probably yours, Dave."

Dave, sitting across from her in the circle, nodded.

"We also saw someone else, paddling solo, in an orange kayak and he was heading west, almost certainly past Gaviota," Katy added.

"Good to know," Theo said.

"You didn't happen to get a photo, did you?" Del asked.

Katy thought for a moment. "No, Miranda was focused on the otters we found near Isla Vista, so her camera would have been pointing the opposite direction."

Dave piped up. "So, we had a bunch of rentals yesterday. After you and Miranda launched, Katy, we did rent to a couple. I've got their names and contact info. Then we rented to a solo guy, so that might be the man you saw in the orange kayak, though other folks rent orange ones, too."

Del's pen continued to move across the pages in his notebook.

"Actually," Dave continued, "I was gonna call the Coast Guard last night, because that renter was late and I was about to close. He called, though, to apologize for being late, said he'd bring in the kayak this morning. When I got to the office, it was already here, washed, no damage, nothing amiss," he reported.

Del spoke up. "Dave, would you know this man if you saw him again?"

"Oh, yeah, I took his rental information personally."

"Can we—Deputy Johnson and I—get that info from you after the meeting?" Theo asked.

"No problem."

"Thanks. He didn't have any distinguishing features you can recall, did he? Especially tall, or muscular, or—"

"The man we saw in the orange kayak was muscular," Katy recalled. "He was very strong, moving fast and paddling like an expert."

"Okay." Del jotted something down.

"And come to think of it," Dave said, "the guy who rented the orange kayak—if it's the same guy—was well built. And he had a mole on his face. A real noticeable one," he added, pointing to his own cheek.

Del's gaze fixed on him. "Think you could work with a sketch artist for us?"

Dave nodded. "I guess so."

Now all eyes were on Del, as though his badge were a billboard advertising law and order. Deferring to the man who'd called the meeting, Del looked at Theo.

"Look," Theo said, understanding the implied question, "we just don't have enough information yet."

"It seems to me we have *plenty* of information," Katy snapped. "An otter has been shot close to a dense population center. The shooter must still be nearby. He or she needs to be apprehended immediately." She sighed. "Sorry. I'm just upset."

Pete reached over to pat her knee.

"Understandable," Del said quietly.

"People who like wildlife and want to watch them up close would never do something like this," Leo observed. "But we do have avid fishers, hunters, applying for licenses all the time."

"Not all fishermen are jerks," Doug remarked.

"I wasn't implying—"

"We're all on the same side here," Theo said, nipping the argument in the bud.

"And we do have a criminal case to solve," Del said, bringing the meeting back to its primary focus.

Theo explained, "Until the necropsy reveals the ordnance and the ballistics can be confirmed, we can't even file a report, let alone request personnel to be assigned to the case. There *is* no case yet, officially."

Katy asked, "The otter that was killed—was she a mother?"

"Yes," Pete replied. "She was lactating."

"Then where's her pup?" Katy demanded, her hands balled into fists. "That has to be my first priority, finding the pup, seeing if we can rescue her—or him."

"We can't stop you from doing your job," Del said, "but I recommend you don't go out alone, at least until we have an investigation under way."

"We can do that," Katy complied.

"Given the gunshot wound was obvious, the necropsy is already under way," said Leo. "I'll be heading over to our lab from here." He looked around the circle. "As you probably know, we don't have a coroner. Instead we have a veterinary pathologist who's examining the carcass to determine cause of death. Usually it'd be parasites, shark bite or algal toxins. Necropsy results give us clues to track down abnormalities in the nearshore ecosystem. This . . . this is entirely different."

"If you contact me as soon as you have results," Theo said, "I can get the process going that much sooner."

"Can do," Leo acceded.

Katy said, "There's at least one person who couldn't get here to the meeting, but he works over on Anacapa."

"Who's that?" asked Del.

"Ken Casmalia. He's a ranger for the brand new National Park."

"I've been wanting to meet him," Del said.

"We all have," Pete echoed. "He's a native. I mean, he's a Native American—he used to be with the Chumash Tribal Council. And he also grew up here, up in Solvang."

"He'll be a welcome addition to the marine community," Katy said. "Smart, experienced, really cares about the region."

"Sounds good," Theo commented.

"So . . ." Dave began, looking around the circle. "How are we going to handle this? We all have to get back to work. Is there a 'party line' we're all going to agree on?"

"Nothing to tell, yet," Doug said.

"Essentially, you're right," Theo said, looking at Doug. "I'd just tell people the law is looking into it. It might be we have a rogue hunter in the area. Any developments in the case will be reported. Something like that."

Dave asked, "And what about if the press starts asking for details?"

"Refer them to my office," Theo replied.

"And if," Del added, "they ask whether this is related to any other open cases, you can refer them to the County Sheriff's office. They know how to deal with the press. And that might take some pressure off you, Theo."

"So you two," Katy said, looking at Theo and Del, "will be working together. But neither of you is exactly local. Will you be working with anyone here, I mean in law enforcement?"

"I'll be making a courtesy call, and keep them informed."

"Something else," Del added, making eye contact with each person in the room. "A note of caution. If you see this man— a guy with a noticeable mole, who's large and muscular—do not make contact. If he approaches *you*, don't offer any hint of recognition. Until we know more, let's assume he's a 'person of interest' and as such, needs to be avoided."

"No reason he'd come back to our shop," Dave said. "He already returned his gear, and if he's the guy, he won't want to be seen."

"True. Even so, just act friendly and pleased to see him. I imagine that's how you'd deal with any other repeat customer."

Dave smiled. "Yeah, pretty much."

Doug said, "Katy, you mentioned Anacapa. We have an excursion planned for tomorrow."

"Right," Katy agreed. "I wasn't thinking about that. Miranda is coming along, you and your tender, right? Is her name Drusilla?"

"Yup."

"And another couple called too," Dave added. "If they're coming, they'll confirm in the morning."

"Wish I could come along," Del said.

"Plenty of room," Doug offered.

"But let's not send up any red flags," Theo cautioned. "Meanwhile, I'll be tracking down whatever leads I can here." After a pause, he looked at Doug. "On the boat tomorrow, will you be topside? Or will you be diving tomorrow?"

"Diving," Doug said.

"Then while you're in the water, perhaps you could take a look to see if anything unusual catches your eye?" Theo asked.

Doug thought for a moment. "I won't be diving for urchins tomorrow, just keeping an eye on our customer who plans to snorkel. So yeah, I can look around."

"And let's hope," Katy said, "you don't find any more dead otters."

31

Miranda Jones wasn't surprised the painting had taken all day.

Sure enough, the imagery of the mural for Zelda's small suite had continued to unroll—both in the artist's mind and on the client's wall—fast and furiously. Usually rather unforgiving, the quick-drying acrylic paint hadn't been a problem today, because Miranda's brush seemed to find the right color, the right stroke, unfailingly.

The cityscape had come first, building from the baseboard molding upward. The patterns of red-tiled roofs over whitewashed buildings began large at the bottom of the image, and grew smaller as they angled diagonally up the lower section of wall, suggesting the perspective that made the image realistic. Next she'd dotted in the tops of trees, and added colorful details like the market umbrellas and awnings she'd noticed from Zelda's balcony.

In the small kitchen area, where a real window showed a section of mountains, she'd painted a continuation of the view, the painted mountains picking up where the real ones were no longer visible. Finally, she'd added that ribbon of ocean arcing westward toward Point Conception, and eastward toward Ventura.

She'd taken breaks a couple of times, to stretch her back, nibble a snack, or grab a tall glass of water. And—to stand back and consider the work in progress. That's when delightful, tiny details would pop into her mind: a futuristic electric car turning a corner; a bright flag flying at the library; a splash of color from bougainvillea climbing a garden wall.

She knew the perspective was slightly unrealistic—a hybrid between a tall rooftop view, and that of a panorama from a helicopter. And the Point Conception Light was located so far down a cliff that from some vantage points it was blocked from view.

In her image, the final sweep of cliffs horseshoed out to the east. And where one might have expected the lighthouse to sit atop the final hump, instead the land dipped dramatically downward and the Light nestled as though on the forelegs of a Sphinx.

From her research, she knew some lighthouses were placed low, like this one, so as to be visible under the low-lying tule fog—a unique California phenomenon that occurred in the winter rainy season and lasted till March. In fact, she'd included some of the cotton-like fog snugged against the mountain of her mural in honor of the fact that she was painting it in February.

Unlike oils, acrylics had no fumes. Still, to give herself a break from the work, she headed downstairs, made some hot tea, and took it out to the balcony. Too chilly to sit without a wrap, she came back inside for her heavy sweater, then resumed her seat and watched as lights winked on across the city. *Wonder if I can see the flash of the lighthouse from here?*

The thought of that flash brought with it the recollection of a dinner with Zackery Calvin at the Milford-Haven Lighthouse Restaurant, an evening that now seemed ages ago, but was actually only last autumn.

How had she felt that night? Excited . . . no, nervous. *Yes, Zack always makes me nervous. Not sure why, but he has from the moment we met.*

He'd knocked on her door, a perfect stranger, who'd found her through Finders Gallery. He'd wanted to buy a painting, but the one he wanted wasn't for sale. So he'd commissioned one like it—or had *said* he wanted to commission her. Then, he hadn't followed through.

After weeks of no contact, he'd resurfaced with an invitation for her to join him backstage at a Doobie Brothers Concert. *I was going to be in Los Angeles then anyway. That was a fantastic night—the excitement of the music, meeting the band.* But again, she'd spent very little time with Zack himself.

Now, here she was in his town, but she had no plans to see him. Some women might have felt comfortable being the one to call him. *Not me. But why?*

She took another sip of her rapidly cooling tea. What did she see in Zack that didn't seem to fit? It was almost as though he was too good a fit in terms of background. Yet Miranda saw herself not as the perfect heiress to her family's fortune, but rather as a black sheep who didn't know what to do with her white privilege. *What are the words to Joni Mitchell's song? I'm a "refugee from a wealthy family."*

Zack, on the other hand, seemed to know exactly what to do with his position. He drove a high-end car, had a glamorous job arranging concerts for celebrity artists, and he came and went at his own whim. None of that made him a bad person. But what, exactly—if anything—did he want from her?

And what do I want? The lighthouse flashed again in the distance, and this time what it brought was an illumination as quick and sharp as the beam of light itself. *I want that flash of insight that says, "I see you. I recognize you."*

Shaking her head, she took her cold tea—and her romantic notion—back inside. She wanted to leave the mural alone for now, and get a good night's sleep. She had another big adventure ahead of her tomorrow.

32

Cedric Worthington stepped into the early morning sunlight of Santa Barbara. He inhaled, already enjoying the walk down State Street toward the water. Last night he and his wife had packed and locked up their house in Santa Maria for the few days they'd be away. Then they'd made the drive south and checked into the Hotel Virginia.

He'd originally planned to find something more economic in nearby Carpenteria, but the Virginia—walking distance from Stearn's Wharf and possessing historic charm—had seemed wiser. The special treat might offset his plans to take his wife on another coastal adventure.

He wandered down the wharf, looking for the D&D Charters sign. When he found it, he saw a tag hung on the door: "Stepped Away. Be Back Soon!"

"Darn," Cedric muttered. But just then, a young man arrived and unlocked the door. "Oh, good! You *are* here."

"Yes, Sir. Sorry about that. Had an early meeting." While he spoke, he began setting brochures out on his counter. Cedric saw that he wore a shirt embroidered with "Dave. D&D Charters."

"Dave, is it?"

"Right."

"One of the owners of D&D?"

"Right again." The young man gave him a wide smile.

"I'd called you about the possibility of joining your trip to Anacapa today."

"Right! Absolutely. Happy to help you with that. Have you been to the Channel Islands before?"

"Nope, this'll be our first time."

Before Cedric returned to his hotel, he'd made plans for a truly exciting day on the water.

Ezmeralda fussed again with the hat, certain that it made her look fat. "Why would you make me wear this thing, anyway?" she complained. "It has a *chin* strap."

"You wouldn't want it to blow off in the wind, Dear," her husband explained. "And I just knew you'd love it because it's your lime green, so it'll go with that favorite purse you have. In any case, I don't want that porcelain skin of yours getting burned."

"Porcelain!" she exclaimed. "More like crackleware at this stage of the game."

"Not to me, Ezme."

She whipped her head around to see whether he was goading her. But seeing his earnest face, her own softened.

She huffed out a breath, then said, "Well, old man, for better or worse, eh?"

"That's the ticket." He beamed.

Companionship, loyalty, longevity—these mattered to him more than snagging a younger woman or keeping his own company. *You'd think I could learn to count my blessings. I try. God knows, I try.*

33

Burt Ostwald had spent a busy day lying low.

The night of the otter attack, he'd managed to climb to safety and have his wounds tended to by an acquaintance in Gaviota—a guy who'd had enough medical training to get him cleaned up, stitched up, and covered up. He didn't want his call to be traceable, so he found a pay phone, made an apology for his tardy equipment return, then added enough excuses to keep the boat rental guy off his neck.

Then he'd returned to the site where he'd stowed the kayak, cleaned it off at a dockside shower, and left it concealed near the front door of D&D Charters.

He'd finally returned to his motel room and holed up with some convenience-store food and some sodas. He'd have preferred beer, but the meds his "doc" had given him were incompatible with alcohol. Between the adrenaline, the injuries, and the exertion, he was exhausted, and fell asleep to the flickering light of the cheap TV in his room at 3 a.m. He'd left a "Do Not Disturb" placard on his door so no maid came by during the day.

Once it was dark again, he woke up, changed his dressings, and went out to grab a couple of burritos, which he ate back in his room. He set the alarm on his watch and slept another few hours, waking at 4 a.m.

As an extra precaution, he packed out all his medical trash—blood-stained bandages could raise a question. Then he put his few belongings in his car and headed up the 101 in the pre-dawn dark.

Offshore, the lights of oil rigs blazed like Christmas trees someone forgot to put away.

He liked the idea of things being forgotten—like dead otters. He hoped that demon-female had sunk to the bottom of the ocean, never to be remembered. As the highway sped by under his tires, he also hoped everyone he'd encountered would soon forget all about him, too.

34

Ezme Worthington stood on the pier and shrieked. "We're getting on *that*!"

"Yes, Dear." Cedric looked around, hoping no one had overheard her complaint. "It's a special charter. The young men who run the company know exactly what they're doing, and they'll do just what we ask. We'll drop anchor, have a lovely lunch, watch some wildlife—"

"How wild is *wild*?" she demanded.

"You know what I mean, native species. Birds, seals, otters—"

"Those horrible, dirty things that poop on the piers?"

"Well, I don't know about pooping. . . ."

"I know what I'm talking about, Cedric. I read up on them. They steal people's oar . . . oar . . . the things that hold the oars in place on rowboats."

"Oarlocks?"

"Exactly. And they smash rocks against boats and ruin the paint. I overheard a woman talking all about it while you were in that office. Isn't that right, young man?"

Dave had just walked down the pier and was making ready to walk across the gangplank. "Uh, well, otters can be pretty crafty." He smiled.

"Nasty is what they can be. I won't have anything to do with them!"

"Well, uh, there are some other people on the trip who might want to watch some otters, but you're welcome to ignore them, Ma'am," Dave reassured her.

"Good! That's exactly what I plan to do. Now, give me a hand walking up that spindly little walkway. We came early so I could get myself settled."

35

Miranda Jones walked down Stearn's Wharf until she found the *Daxwell*, one of the three boats owned by D&D Charters. The size and shape reminded her of the *Seatacean* in Morro Bay, a whale-watching boat on which she'd had a grand adventure a few months earlier.

She glanced up and saw that people were already aboard making preparations for today's excursion to Anacapa. Since everyone was too busy to stop what they were doing and usher her aboard, she walked up the narrow gangway, then called "Permission to come aboard?"

"Permission granted," a female voice replied, its owner's head popping out from the entrance to the below-decks area.

When Miranda arrived on the aft deck, the blonde greeted her, compact body tightly wrapped in jeans and T-shirt, hair in a French braid, and a shy smile. "Drusilla," she said, extending her hand. "Folks call me Dru."

"Dru. Great. Good to meet you."

"I work for Doug Haliwell, the other half of D&D. I know you've met Dave. Doug should be here soon. They had a meeting this morning."

"Guess they start early," Miranda commented.

"Always. So, you can stow your gear below."

"Okay, got it. Thanks." Miranda headed "below." *Love that expression. I remember hearing it when I first embarked on the* Planet Peace *voyage. Makes me feel like a real mariner, though I'm hardly that.*

36

Doug Haliwell stood at the *Daxwell*'s helm, keeping the boat to a slightly slower velocity so as to give his passengers as smooth a ride as possible, given the light chop in the Santa Barbara Channel. The crossing would take them through some of the busiest shipping lanes on the California coast, and Doug paid close attention to boat traffic, and creatures.

"Hope there are no military exercises today," Dru said, loudly enough to be heard over the sound of both waves and engine.

"Military?" Miranda asked.

"Big military history around here. There was a Marine Corps Air Station in Goleta during World War II. These days there's Vandenberg, the Air Force Base in Lompoc, out near Point Conception. They hold this competition called the

Guardian Challenge. I know about it because my brother's a flyer. This year—'97—is the thirtieth anniversary of the competition and also the fiftieth anniversary of the Air Force. So it's a big deal for them."

"Must be! I didn't realize there was an Air Force base so close to here."

"They do all kinds of military exercises of course. But they also help with fire fighting when the city or the county needs them."

"Thank God."

"Yeah."

Miranda fell silent for a moment, enjoying the surge of the boat through the waves, the whip of the wind, the tang of the sea spray. Then, once again working to lift her voice above the noise, she asked, "What got you interested in tending on a fishing boat?"

Dru smiled. "I was working on my PhD at UCSB and got tired of the politics."

Miranda knew the surprise showed clearly on her own face when she said, "Wow, talk about packing a lot into one sentence! So . . . is it Doctor Dru, then?"

"Yes. But don't tell anyone." Dru laughed.

Miranda shook her head. "Something to do with the ocean?"

"Marine Science Graduate Program. I loved the studies, just couldn't stand the positioning, and the prospect of facing years of pressure to publish."

"So . . . what will you do with your degree?" Miranda wondered.

"Not sure yet. But I have time. Right now, I just love getting the practical experience of being on the water, learning a trade, observing all the sea life up close. I found some good company, too," she added, glancing behind her at Doug.

Now it was Miranda who smiled. "Aha, that kind of good company."

"Not that he has a clue," Dru observed. "It's okay. Like I said, I have time."

Miranda grinned, then looked out across the water, wondering if and when she'd ever have a relationship about which she could feel so sure, and so patient.

A few minutes later, Miranda watched as Dru and Doug traded places. *He may not realize it yet, but he trusts her.* She saw Dru cup her hand and speak into his ear, then watched as a cat-that-ate-the-canary smile took over his face. *That man doesn't have a chance. Dru gave him the bait and she's reeling him in, and all the while he still thinks he's swimming free.*

Miranda wiped the grin off her face when Doug came toward her, asked whether she wanted to follow him below. "Sure," she said, relieved when they made their way to the galley, away from the noise of the wind.

"I just wanted to go over our plans for today," Doug said, sitting across from her.

"Great, I appreciate it."

"So, you and Katy Sails kayaked around, observed otters in the kelp near shore. Today you plan to snorkel, right?"

"Yes, I wanted to see them under water, understand better how they move. I've only seen them bobbing at the surface."

Doug nodded. "While you snorkel, I'll be diving. With my

SCUBA gear, I'll be able to keep open for any predators that might be swimming by."

"Oh! Oh. I hadn't thought about that."

"I really don't expect trouble. Just rather be safe."

Miranda took a deep breath. "By all means! I certainly appreciate that!"

Doug Haliwell spent a few minutes explaining some of the creatures they were likely to see today, then looked up as Katy came below and sat beside Miranda.

Apparently unconcerned about discussing otter behavior from his perspective in front of an otter rescuer, Doug continued. "Even though the otters are popular among environmentalists and tourists, they're voracious eaters. They're pretty much the worst nightmare not only for urchin divers, like me, but also for folks who harvest abalone, and for that matter lobsters and squid. We're very careful with what we take, in terms of size and quality. The otters? They take any and everything. And they don't even eat it all. They tear up their food, drop a lot of it back in the water, so it just goes to waste. It's hard to see half a valuable urchin drifting down to the bottom."

Katy—polite and wise enough to have let Doug have his say—pointed out, "It's a very complicated situation that started way back when sea otters were hunted to the brink of extinction. While the otters were pretty much missing from the ecosystem, the urchins really had to be held in check, lest they destroy all the kelp forests. Commercial fishing developed as a viable industry, and everyone was happy. Sort of. Until that small colony of sea otters was discovered and put on the Endangered Species list, and started to make enough of a comeback that now, they threaten the fishing industry."

Miranda looked from one new friend to the other, glimpsing how challenging it was for them to be on opposite sides of the otter issue. "So, I've heard about the 'No Otter Zone' but I don't quite understand it."

Doug huffed. "Doubt anyone can."

"Yeah, it does seem rather absurd," Katy put in. "Some say it came about because of pressure from the oil companies. They have off-shore rigs here, and in the event of another spill—even though it's been years since they had one—they don't want the bad press and public outcry from killing otters, whose pelts are sensitive to the least amount of grease and debris."

"But it wasn't the oil companies who created the 'zone,'" Doug protested. "It was the U.S. Fish and Wildlife Service that exported a group of otters to San Nicolas, and tried to establish a colony there. They thought it'd keep otters away from the coastal region, but they just swam back."

"Or they tried to," Katy added. "A lot of them disappeared, probably killed by shark. So the new colony was a failure. And now there are all kinds of lawsuits. So no one knows exactly what'll happen."

Ken Casmalia had been keeping to himself, riding the bow and enjoying the journey. Each time he came out to the NPS station on Anacapa he could feel himself disengaging from the tribal politics in Santa Inez and tuning in to the islands. The history of his people was everywhere in the region—islands and coastal areas alike—but on the islands he could hear the whisperings of ancestors who never seemed to have left. He'd given up dismissing the sensation of their presence, so now, he made an effort to consider what they might expect of him.

When it came to communicating with non-tribal members, he felt his primary job was to teach without pontificating, to share the ancient culture that preceded Europeans by thousands of years without adding an attitude of superiority, which could easily defeat the purpose of good will and mutual respect. It all sometimes weighed on him like a burden, but then it would lift off him, drifting away as easily as fog clearing off the islands. Then he remembered the privilege of the office and tried to stay focused on that.

When he felt a hand on his shoulder, he startled and, turning his head, found himself looking at a woman he hadn't met.

"Mr. Casmalia?"

He nodded.

"I'm Miranda Jones. I'm an artist, here to do some paintings and sketches of sea otters. Katy Sails hired me, and she's been my tour guide, I guess you could say."

"Miranda Jones . . . I've heard of you. Seen some of your paintings." *She wasn't on the faxed list of who'd be at the meeting. Better not mention it.*

"Really?" The woman seemed a little embarrassed.

"Finders Gallery in Milford-Haven. Beautiful work."

"Thank you. I thought you were going to say you knew my friend Kuyama, because you and she are both—"

"On the Tribal Council. Yes, she's my very good friend," he agreed.

"Then we have something wonderful in common. She's my good friend, too."

The distance he'd felt between himself and this stranger

suddenly closed and he settled into a sense of ease. "Now that you say that, I recall her speaking about her painter friend. In fact, she said something about you. What was it?"

"Oh, dear, something good I hope," Miranda said.

"Oh yeah, it was about your eyes. Not your actual eyes, but the way you see things."

"That is the job, when it comes down to it," Miranda concurred. "You have to see it before you can paint it."

As the conversation reached a pause, they both turned to face the islands, most of their outlines still shrouded in fog. But just then, the painter pointed.

"Look at that patch of yellow!" she called. "Has to be clusters of coreopsis. It blooms this time of year. Oh, my! It's so odd. I can't even see the islands clearly yet, but I can see the colors."

"You *do* have painter eyes," Ken said, feeling himself smile. "We should see some red paintbrush too—in honor of our visiting painter."

Miranda laughed.

"This time of year we have a rainbow of blooming native wildflowers. And the rainbow ... it's one of our tribal symbols."

"Oh, how lovely," Miranda commented. "Look, the island is ... well, I thought I saw it for a moment. It's drifting in and out of view."

"The Native word *Anypakh* means deception or mirage," he explained.

"That's the original name for Anacapa?"

"Right. It seems to change shape when viewed at different times from the mainland and other islands."

"There must be so much to learn about these islands."

That was his opening, and he felt he could push the virtual

door open a little further. "Anacapa itself is actually three islets called East, Middle, and West. And that forty-foot–high Arch Rock you'll see when we arrive at the Landing Cove on East Anacapa? It's the symbol of Anacapa and of the Park."

"Of course it is," Miranda said, apparently cataloging the information for future reference.

"That's part of my spiel, by the way." Ken glanced at his watch. "And I'll be giving it a bit later today. They'll send a skiff out to pick me up, once the *Daxwell* is anchored."

"Well, I hope to hear the whole thing someday. I'll have to come back when I can spend more time."

"Kayak through the caves, climb to the lighthouse, hike the trails. Happy to be your guide."

She smiled. "That's an offer I won't forget."

37

Miranda Jones wriggled one more time, hoping the wet suit would feel more comfortable, then resigned herself to the fact she'd just have to get used to it. Katy had already assured her the suit was a good fit, and also warned her that, without it, she'd only be able to stay in the water for a very few minutes. *This time of year... I hadn't realized how cold it'd be. She said September was warmer, because summer sun warmed the water for three months.* Still, "warm" was a relative term.

Doug stood waiting for her on the swimmers' deck—a lip at the stern, below the main deck and hovering just above the water line. He was already suited up, had his fins on, and was ready to lower his mask and put the SCUBA regulator in his mouth.

"All set?" he asked, a note of tension in his voice.

Is he irritated with me? Or maybe just impatient, Miranda wondered, then immediately replied, "I think so."

"Okay, just follow me at first, okay? I'll lead you over to the kelp. I've already located a raft of otters. Then, when Katy joins us in a few minutes, I'll dive, keep an eye on things at depth."

"Perfect." Miranda lowered her own mask, put the snorkel mouthpiece in place, and sat down. Once her fins were on, she scooched off the platform and slid into the silky water, heart beating faster as her adventure began.

Miranda'd been swimming for several minutes, enjoying the view through her mask as she breathed through her snorkel. To take a break and clear moisture from the tube, she brought her head up just in time to see Katy arrive by kayak.

Miranda swam to her, and held lightly to the side of the familiar kayak. "Hi. Oh, this is amazing," she said, once her mouthpiece was set aside. "Just watching the kelp stipes wave is beautiful. The length of them descends beyond line of sight, as if I'm swimming in a tree canopy."

"Basically, that's what you *are* doing," Katy put in.

Katy's usually sunny disposition seemed to have deserted her. Just like Doug. Maybe they had an argument?

"Are you warm enough?"

Katy's question interrupted Miranda's musings. "Barely," she admitted.

"Okay, I'll be close by. Just swim over and climb in any time you want to get out of the water. I've got an extra paddle for you."

"Okay, thanks."

"Meanwhile, I'm gonna be keeping an eye open for a particular otter who I think will have had her pup by now."

"Oh, yeah? How will you know her? White nose scar?"

"Yes, and in the shape of a heart."

"Really? Fantastic!" Miranda exclaimed. "I'll look for her too."

"Great," Katy said. "Have fun," she added almost as an afterthought.

Before swimming away, Miranda glanced back to the *Daxwell*, where she noticed an older couple standing at the stern rail. *Odd . . . I didn't know there were other passengers.* She couldn't see their faces clearly enough to tell whether they looked familiar. But what she did see was a woman wearing a neon-lime hat with a matching fabric bag slung over her shoulder. The color reminded her of a woman she'd seen twice before on ocean adventures—a woman she'd given the name "Mrs. Lime" in honor of the intrusive color. *But of course, she wouldn't be on a trip like this, especially after her complaints about the whale-watching excursion.*

Dismissing the thought, Miranda turned back to watch as Katy paddled toward the closest raft of otters.

Cedric Worthington inhaled deeply the delights of the sea air, and enjoyed the sway of the *Daxwell*'s deck under his feet. Ezmeralda finally felt well enough to climb up to the main deck. Despite the medication she'd taken, she'd still gotten seasick again, which was discouraging. During their hour-long crossing to Anacapa, he'd repeatedly suggested she might find the sea air refreshing, but she'd refused to do anything but cling to a handle on the bulkhead closest to built-in seating below deck, deep in the prow, a bucket close at hand.

"Hold onto the rail, Dear," he suggested when she emerged,

blinking as her eyes adjusted to the bright sunlight. "You won't believe the view of the island. Did you ever see so many wild flowers?"

"We see them every spring, Cedric, on the hillside right below our house. What's so special about these?"

"They're just gorgeous, if you ask me, fading in and out of those low clouds."

"Those are not clouds. That's fog. And that means we could get socked in and stuck way out here a hundred miles away from civilization." She shuddered. "And it's cold."

"Less than fifty, Dear. And here, take my sweater. I'm not chilly at all," he said, sliding out of his cardigan to slip it over her shoulders and drape it over the purse that bulged at her side.

"Well, that's a little better," Ezme conceded.

At last, a trace of a smile. Progress, he thought. "You know, you could leave your purse below decks. I'll be happy to take it back down for you."

"Heavens, no!" Ezme objected. "What if I need something? No, the purse stays with me."

"You would know best. Now, let's walk to the stern and watch for a few minutes. There's someone kayaking, and someone else diving."

"Well, I'm sure I can't imagine why anyone would want to get into the frigid water, but if that's what you want to look at, I suppose we might as well."

Cedric looked up to see tendrils of fog skidding across the vivid yellow flowers clinging to the high cliffs. Then his gaze followed a chain of pelicans as they streamed out over the gleaming water. He stood on the fandeck, one arm around his wife, one hand holding the rail, and watched as one young woman managed to bounce herself into the kayak where another young woman already sat.

When he chuckled, Ezme asked, "What's so funny?"

"Oh, those two gals. In their wetsuits, they look like little orcas paddling a kayak."

Ezme squinted, then pronounced, "Neither one of them has the sense God gave a sea gull. They've dressed themselves like those sea otters. And there aren't two of them, there are three."

Cedric focused again on the kayak. "Three?" Sure enough, a third body had joined the two women in their kayak.

Miranda hoisted herself into the kayak and took the aft seat. "Nice going," Katy observed.

"Let me just stow my mask and snorkel and get my fins off," Miranda said, a little out of breath.

"Okay, but I think we're getting some company," Katy said.

"What?"

At that moment, an otter poked a curious nose near the bow, pulled itself right up onto the kayak, then landed to settle across Katy's shins.

"Oh my!" Miranda exclaimed.

"Hi there, fella," Katy greeted their visitor with a soothing tone. "Did you come to say hello?"

The young otter blinked at Katy, then turned around to nibble at her neoprene booties.

"I don't suppose those taste very good, do they?" she remarked.

As if in reply, the otter squealed, then nestled again comfortably between her legs.

Miranda, eager to observe, leaned forward and watched over Katy's shoulders. "Wish I had my camera," she said quietly.

"You'll remember," Katy said, "and draw him. That'll be even better."

Departing just as quickly as he'd arrived, their visitor slid off the other side of the kayak and disappeared from view.

Miranda pushed back to her seat and had barely recovered her balance when the otter popped its head up next to her, used its paws to grasp the edge of the kayak, then plopped itself on her lap. "Oh! He's . . . he's heavy. I shouldn't try to pet him, right?"

"No, don't," Katy confirmed. "Just let him explore."

"Right."

Now the otter sampled Miranda's booties, but, apparently dissatisfied with the taste, circled as a puppy might, snuggled between her lower legs, and rested his head on her thigh, gazing up at her with an alert, curious expression. "You're adorable, and precious, aren't you?" Miranda said. And with a quick nod, the otter moved his sleek body and slid over the side.

Enchanted by their visitor, Miranda also noted the pup had managed to restore Katy's cheerful mood. *After all, who could resist that baby-charm?*

Ezme Worthington took a gulp of air. "Good Lord!" she yelled. "Those girls are going to be eaten alive!"

"No, no, Dear," Cedric reassured her. "Those are sea otters, and they eat abalones and urchins, not people."

"They're disgusting!" she declared. "And those teeth are plenty sharp to do plenty of damage. Serves those girls right for being out there where they don't belong."

"But that's what they do, Dear, they study the otters. I mean, one of them does. She rescues them, actually."

"Well, that's the stupidest thing I ever heard. A person rescuing a sea otter? They don't need rescuing! It's the girls who need to be rescued! There are terrible reports, you know, about injuries from otter bites."

"You're thinking of river otters, Ezme. They're territorial, so when people get too close, they defend their territory."

"Well, whose territory do you think those girls are in?"

Because his wife had a point, Cedric fell silent.

Miranda Jones paddled smoothly behind Katy as they progressed quietly toward the bevy of otters. Some were banging abalone shells on their chest, some were chewing eagerly, some slid under water to dive for their next meal. And one mom diligently groomed the small pup napping on her belly.

"I think that's her," Katy said quietly.

"The heart-otter?" Miranda asked.

"Yes. Cory, we named her."

"Oh, perfect. 'Core' for heart?"

"You're quick," Katy remarked. "I just want to drift here for a moment to see if she'll turn her head."

They waited, their kayak slipping through strands of kelp, their eyes focused on the otter mom.

"It is her," Katy said, excitement bubbling up into her voice. "Hi, Cory," she called gently to the otter. "Good to see you."

The otter's head swung immediately in their direction, and Miranda felt certain she'd recognized Katy's voice. What the otter would do next, she waited anxiously to see. *Will she feel threatened because of her pup? Will she swim away? Will she approach?*

The otter didn't do any of the things Miranda had predicted, but simply resumed her grooming.

"Good," Katy said quietly. "She doesn't feel threatened. So we can just stay here for a while."

Miranda found the repetitive movements soothing and almost hypnotic, but then she was startled to hear Katy sniffle and clear her throat. "You're not upset about something, are you?" she asked.

"I'm okay," Katy replied defensively, then she swung into instructress mode. "It's kind of too bad we missed the really newborn stage. The pup seems about a week old. You'd be surprised how mobile they are at such a young age. But this is still a great opportunity to watch close up."

As they waited and watched, they failed to notice that a current was carrying them closer to the *Daxwell*.

Cedric Worthington watched as a speedboat streaked across the water, lifting a white V-shaped wake that turned into a wave traveling the far side of the landing bay in which the *Daxwell* was anchored. Though he knew the wave would eventually reach them and bobble the kayakers as well as the otters they watched, he couldn't imagine any damage would be done. And he knew their own boat would just waggle for a moment, then steady on the calm sea.

His wife huffed out a breath next to him. "Standing in the sun like this, I'm getting too hot," she complained.

"You could take off my sweater, Dear," Cedric suggested.

"If I do I'll probably be too cold. But what other choice do I have?"

As the question was rhetorical, Cedric didn't answer, but simply helped as she struggled out of his sweater.

"I'll take that," she said. "I might want it later." She turned to receive the garment from him. In the process, her purse straps slid off her shoulder and caught at her elbow—evidently an annoying impediment. So she drew her arm out of the straps to balance the bag on the rail—just wide enough to hold the purse— freeing her hands to fold his sweater.

"Hmm, not sure you want to put your purse there, Ezme. We wouldn't want it to—"

But his words and his outstretched hand were too late. The wake reached the *Daxwell*, which shuddered just enough to tip the bag over the rail and onto the swimming step several feet below.

"Aaaackkkk!" Ezme shrieked, and a gust of wind carried the sound out over the water.

Katy Sails turned her head at the sound of a woman's scream, fearing that someone had fallen overboard off the *Daxwell*.

She saw two passengers standing at the rail, but no one made wild gestures, no alarm sounded, and no rescue oper-ation seemed to be in progress. Katy also now realized that the speedboat's wake had pushed them—kayakers and otters alike—much closer to the boat.

"What's that?" she asked Miranda, pointing at the bright green object on the swimmers' step.

"Oh, dear," Miranda said. "I think that's a purse."

Whatever it was, it had drawn the attention of Cory's

pup, who now slipped off his mother's abdomen with a high-pitched squeak, making a bee-line for it.

With an answering squeal, the otter mom rolled over and pursued the pup, but with quick agility, he'd already bounded up onto the step.

*

Dru MacIntosh heard a woman screaming and came running to the aft deck, where she tried to determine what might be the cause of their passenger's panic.

"Her purse!" Mr. Worthington yelled in order to be heard over his wife's shrieks. And then he pointed overboard.

Dru looked over the stern rail and couldn't help but laugh when she saw the cutest otter pup she'd ever seen cavorting with a collapsed ball of green fabric. *Not a ball . . . that must be the woman's bag. Oh, dear.*

Deftly hoisting herself over the rail and down the short ladder, Dru was about to land on the aft slip to see if she could rescue the bag, when she caught sight of the otter mom virtually flying across the water and directly . . . at *her*! Boosting herself back up the ladder, she was only just in time to avoid the sharp claws of the otter now determined to protect her offspring.

If Mrs. Worthington's screams had been loud before, now they reached operatic proportions. With this cacophony underscoring the scene before her, Dru watched as more players arrived on the set of this improvised drama.

*

Doug Haliwell checked his perimeter again. Diving shallow—only about ten feet below the surface—he'd been keeping an eye on the kayak and on the otters diving through the kelp. So far, there'd been no predators lurking.

What he did notice was a disturbance that could only have been caused by a speedboat moving fast enough to send a wave that not only traveled through the bay, but pushed the kayak and at least one otter group closer to the *Daxwell*, whose stern and screw he could see through the clear water.

Love this, he thought. *Floating in the quiet. Watching the life under the surface, an entire world of its own.* He kicked gently, his fins propelling him with ease. *So, yesterday I'm fighting otters for urchin. Today, I'm protecting otters from natural enemies. No one can say I have a dull job. Hope nothing too exciting happens before our clients make it safely back aboard.*

Then a flash of movement caught his peripheral vision. *Damn! I must've spoken too soon.*

Miranda Jones heard Katy call out, "He's trapped!"

"What?" she asked. Their kayak was now close enough to the *Daxwell* that another stroke or two would bring them alongside the swim step. But Katy began to back-peddle.

And now, Miranda glanced up just in time to see why. Cory the otter mom virtually flew out of the water, aiming herself at Dru, who managed to propel herself up and over the rail, the otter missing her by a whisker.

But all this drama had distracted Miranda—and everyone else—from the urgent matter Katy had seen. The pup, evidently thrilled with the bright green bag, had slid himself inside. Now, neither he nor his mom could extricate him.

"What can we do?" Miranda asked, yelling to be heard over the screams of someone on the rear deck of the *Daxwell*.

She glanced up. "Oh, no! It *is* her!" How Mrs. Lime could have popped up yet again, was too much for Miranda to process at this point. Instead, she leaned forward so as to be able to hear Katy more clearly.

"Cory is panicked, so she's dangerous. But we'll have to get the pup out of the bag, because he could drown."

Fortunately, Doug surfaced just then. He clung to the kayak while he removed his regulator, then asked, "What's all the commotion?"

"Otter pup is trapped in that bag. It's got stuff in it . . . obviously heavy enough to sink. Pup's keeping it afloat, for now."

"That explains why I saw the mom bulleting this way under water," he said, sliding his mask to the top of his head. "And who the hell is screaming?"

Dru made one more effort at calming Mrs. Worthington, who simply would not be silenced. Giving up, she turned to the husband. "Please, can you get her away from the rear deck? I know Doug and Katy are trying to rescue that pup. The screaming isn't helping."

Nodding, Mr. Worthington grasped Ezme by the shoulders and bustled her away.

Cory felt each squeal of her pup ricochet through her body, each sound biting into her more viciously than any mate had ever done.

Must save!

He only wanted to play, she knew. And she'd had an innate

fear of the human-object that had attracted his baby-mind's attention.

Still too young!

Her heart hammered in her chest as she watched his movements through the green thing, his little paws too small to grasp its edges.

Her own paws grasped at the thing, but she only managed to pull it away from the boat, where it sank a few inches below the surface.

Out! Must get him out!

And now . . . now there were more humans.

Must protect!

"Cory!"

She heard the human-voice, knew its sound. For one moment, she turned toward it.

Miranda sat in the kayak, watching as these two otter experts each thought through the possibilities.

Then, Katy spoke first. "I think I can get the pup out of the bag, if Miranda will help. But—"

Before Miranda could chime in, Doug said, "But I'll need to distract the mother."

"Exactly," Katy said. "I know, it's asking a lot. I'm the otter rescuer, and you're the . . . Well, you don't necessarily love the otters like I do. And she could hurt you."

Doug held her gaze.

"I think she knows me, knows my voice. So I could try to keep her away. But I'm not sure anyone else could handle the pup."

"Doug!"

Miranda, Katy and Doug all looked toward the boat, where Dru was leaning over the rail waving something long and metallic.

Evidently Doug understood immediately what Dru wanted. When she gestured toward the starboard side of the boat, Doug slid his mask on again, said "Be right back," and stuck the regulator in his mouth. Quicker than Miranda would have thought possible, he swam towards mid-ships on the starboard side, then reached up, while Dru leaned as far over as she could, handing him the tool she carried. Doug asked her something Miranda couldn't hear. Then Doug swam back to the kayak.

"Okay," he said, once he'd removed his regulator. Taking a couple of deep breaths, he explained. "My urchin rake. It'll give me a chance to prod the otter mom if I have to, keep her better than arm's length away."

"So you'll be okay dealing with Cory," Katy said.

"Timing will be critical," Doug said, ignoring Katy's concern. "Miranda, if you can grab the bag itself, just hold it away from your body. Then, Katy, you should be able to reach inside for the pup. You'll know where to grab him, how to hold him."

"Right," Katy agreed.

"Dru is gonna throw down some food. Whatever seafood we had in the fridge. That should catch the mom's attention for a few seconds. That's probably all the time you'll have. But I'll keep her away as long as I can."

"Miranda and I will have to be in the water. Can't handle the kayak and the pup," Katy thought out loud. "I could throw Dru a line to secure the kayak."

"Good, she can do that. Soon as she throws down the bag of food."

"Right," Katy agreed.

The three of them made eye contact. Then Katy put on her fins and mask. Miranda followed, her heart kicking against her chest. A few moments later, the agreed-upon sequence of actions began: Miranda slipped into the water; Doug swam toward the swim step; Dru dropped the bag of food to him, and reached out to catch the line Katy threw in her direction; Katy went over the side of the kayak.

Miranda watched as Doug banged the edge of the step, then ripped open the bag of shrimp Dru had thrown. The otter mom's head swung toward him immediately, her upper body rising out of the water as she held both paws up. *Like she's wearing boxing gloves,* Miranda thought, too nervous to be amused at the sight.

"Now!" Katy said.

Miranda grabbed the closed end of the sodden green bag, feeling the pup wriggling inside.

It took Katy several seconds to clear the straps out of the way and find the bag's opening. When she did, both hands grasped the wiggly, sleek little body of the precious pup.

Yet this was not the time for elation, for this could be the most dangerous moment—if Cory thought Katy was stealing her pup.

From Miranda's vantage point—just a few feet away, her head just above water level—everything seemed to happen in slow motion. Doug held out the bag of shrimp toward Cory, who seemed about to grab for it, when she heard the squeals of her pup no longer muffled by the sodden bag. Flipping herself toward her pup, Cory plunged toward Katy, who meanwhile had carefully placed the pup on the swim step, then back-stroked away.

Mom and pup were united in an ecstasy of sound and motion. Cory's paws sped over the soft pelt of her beloved pup, while his little paws pulled at her coat in eager relief. All the while, the two sang to each other in squeals of delight.

Then Cory, holding her baby in a tight embrace, brought her head up, making eye contact with each of her rescuers by turns. The pup, apparently sensing he should follow his mother's lead, stared at each of the humans as she did.

Miranda stared back, letting the moment burn into her memory: the relief on Cory's face as the white heart seemed to pulse on her nose; the smug comfort in the pup's expression. To Miranda, there was no doubt at all that the otters were thanking them.

38

Katy Sails, her mask on top of her head, couldn't stop the tears from cascading down her face, nor could she stop herself from laughing.

"It's okay," she reassured Doug and Miranda. "I'm just sort of overwhelmed. Wow. Go team!"

The three of them, still afloat near the swim step, formed a circle and held each other's forearms for a moment.

Katy was the first to hoist herself onto the step and start removing her fins. Miranda followed. But when it was Doug's turn, he hesitated.

All of them could hear the continuing wails of the woman who'd started the crisis.

"There is the matter of her purse," Doug said through clenched teeth. "I suppose I could take a look, see if I can retrieve it."

"Oh, that'd be so good," Katy said.

Without another word, Doug pulled his mask down, stuck the regulator in his mouth, and jackknifed below the surface.

"You never know," Katy said to Miranda. "He might find it."

Miranda shook her head. "It's sure bright enough."

The two broke into fits of laughter, then tried to tone it down, lest the woman overhear.

Dru appeared above them, leaning over the rail. "He's diving for it, isn't he?" she said, though it wasn't really a question.

Miranda and Katy had just nodded, when Doug popped to the surface and flung the soggy mass of lime green fabric onto the step. "Nothing in it, of course. But there it is. I'm going down one more time, see if I spot a wallet, or anything."

"What a guy," Miranda said to Dru.

"You know it," she said, a tender expression on her face.

When he next reappeared, he whipped off his mask and regulator. "Nope," he said. "Couldn't find anything else."

"Sure was nice of you to try," Dru called down to him.

Dru MacIntosh watched as Doug, still wearing his wet suit and still dripping ocean water, carried the purse toward the portside rail, where Mrs. Worthington still complained bitterly to her husband.

"Mrs. Worthington?" Doug interrupted.

"What!" she said.

"For what it's worth, here's your bag," he offered, holding it out to her.

Mrs. Worthington looked down at the soggy fabric. "Did you recover my credit cards?"

"Uh, no. I did another dive in case I could find anything

that might have been inside. Anyway, maybe you can still do something with the bag itself."

"Does your insurance cover my intolerable loss?" she demanded.

"You'd, uh, have to discuss that with Dave when we get back," he said, obviously struggling to keep his temper in check.

The husband stepped in. "We do thank you very much, young man. It was very kind of you to get it back for us."

"It was not kind," Mrs. Worthington objected. "It was his job."

Forcing air past his inflated cheeks, Mr. Worthington said, "He's doing his job, Dear, and doing it very well."

Doug nodded, and walked away, his neoprene bootie-clad feet squishing across the deck, leaving a trail of puddles.

Dru didn't know which she wanted to do more—slap Mrs. What's-her-name, or kiss Doug; but the latter sounded like a much better idea.

Miranda Jones had followed the others in changing into dry clothes and stowing her gear for the trip back to the mainland.

Everyone gathered, now, around the large galley table below decks, including a subdued Mrs. Worthington. Dru had heated enough water to make a huge pot of tea, and she handed plastic mugs to Katy, who passed them to the others.

Miranda had her small sketchpad on the table, her hand moving quickly to capture images from their recent adventure while they were still so fresh in her mind.

"Wish I could do that," Katy said wistfully.

"She's got the gift," Dru added, as Doug nodded.

Though Miranda heard what they were saying, she'd tuned their comments to a low volume so she could continue sketching. A few minutes later, she paused, and looked around at the group quietly sipping their mugs of tea.

Thank goodness Mrs. Lime has finally quieted down. She was getting on everyone's last nerve.

Just then, the woman's hand reached across the table to grab Miranda's sketchpad. Mrs. Worthington turned it around and flipped through the fresh pages. "Otters don't look like that, you know," she pronounced.

Miranda was too startled to reply, and so, it seemed, was everyone else.

"No, no, they don't," Mrs. "Lime" continued. "They're longer and they look more like weasels. I could tell that when I watched that creature climb all over you in the kayak."

Taking a deep breath, Miranda replied quietly, "You're thinking of river otters. And you're right, their heads, their bodies are shaped differently from sea otters."

Mrs. Worthington continued as though Miranda hadn't spoken. "They're vicious, you know. I was telling my husband."

"Not usually. Not unless they think someone's threatening them, or their pup."

"An otter is an otter is an otter, my girl. You'll learn one day."

Miranda pressed her lips together. Doug looked about ready to hurl his mug, and the other folks seemed to be holding their breath.

Trying to frame a reply, Miranda looked at Mrs. Worthington's face and realized the woman was about to tear up again.

"What will I do?" she wailed softly. "I've lost everything, even my beautiful gold compact!"

"Actually, just think," Miranda offered. "Now you get to go shopping for a new wallet, a new make-up case, and . . . a whole new purse! I bet you'll find one even better than the one you lost."

"Well, I wouldn't go that far," Mrs. Worthington complained, her upset already subsiding. "And I'll still have to go around to all my favorite shops and get new loyalty cards, replace my credit cards, and Lord knows how long I'll have to stand in line to get a new driver's license!"

"Yes, all that is a terrible bother," Miranda agreed.

"Still, you had a good thought." Turning to her husband, she said, "Ceddie! You're going to take me shopping at some swanky store in Santa Barbara!"

The sudden exuberance seemed to break the impending doom and gloom, and everyone burst out laughing. Mr. Worthington looked at Miranda with a mixture of gratitude and resignation, no doubt realizing he'd soon be taking his wife shopping in one of the most expensive towns in the region.

39

Miranda Jones reveled in the quiet relief of being back in her own home.

She'd stopped by her friend Kevin's house to pick up her cat. The moment Miranda opened her car door, Shadow leaped out to land on the front lawn and streak toward the front entrance. As Miranda unlocked it, Shadow used her full vocal register to indicate her impatience at getting inside.

"I know how you feel, Girl. I'm eager to be home, too."

After all the bags were dragged inside, the painting supplies stacked in her studio, and her suitcase taken downstairs to her bedroom, Miranda made herself a cup of tea, then settled on her couch with her quilt wrapped around her legs. As Shadow curled up on her lap, Miranda looked out the sliding glass door where the sun was just setting on a chilly afternoon in Milford-Haven.

After her adventurous trip to Anacapa, she'd spent almost an-other full week in Santa Barbara, with five days outlining, then painting the exterior mural for Sea Otter Rescue. Katy Sails had been so thrilled, she'd thrown Miranda a group dinner at Sand Castle Café that included Dru and Doug, and Dave from D&D Charters. They'd dined on a delectable assortment of fried clams, fried shrimp, fish-and-chips, and cole slaw, wash-ing it all down with sodas or beers, and all promising to stay in touch.

On her final day in town, Miranda'd put the finishing touches on Zelda's interior mural, then removed all her paint-ing supplies. Before she left the next day, she cleaned the rooms she'd used and left a nice note. She smiled at the thought of Zelda returning home and heading immediately upstairs to in-spect her new room, expecting she'd hear from her when that happened.

Late on the morning of Valentine's Day, Miranda had driven south, taking the 101 to Los Angeles, more courageous in the wild flow of L.A. traffic since she'd braved it during her adven-ture last winter, a trip for painting assignments that'd taken her from Palos Verdes and the San Vicente Lighthouse, to the Hollywood Bowl, to the Mojave Desert.

This time when she transferred to the 405, she felt almost like a native, but then found herself in unfamiliar territory again on the 5 until she drove through San Diego to a mod-est hotel near the San Diego Zoo. After checking in, she had enough time to rest, shower, and dress for the Gala.

As she slid on the slinky red dress, she realized her Mother'd been absolutely right. It clung to her curves, yet wasn't too revealing. Miranda loved the simple lines and it felt comfortable—something she found out later could not be said about gowns worn by a lot of other women at the affair. The color proved to be perfect for the occasion and made her feel more at home as she found herself in a sea of ruby and burgundy dresses, scarlet and wine bow-ties and cummerbunds.

Though sitting at one of the head tables and being recognized from the podium made her uncomfortable, still she had much more fun than she'd expected to. And she couldn't help but be pleased her work had been appreciated and helped raise money for the zoo's Wild Animal Park, where the animals roamed free and the humans visited by vehicle.

A high point of the evening was being seated next to Dr. Roger Payne, the great zoologist and discoverer of whale song. His recordings—captured from his microphone draped over the side of his boat—became the source material for his many years of study and gradually became part of both the environmental movement and pop culture, when he released *Songs of the Humpback Whale*—which became the best-selling nature sound recording ever.

Miranda's own love of whales had started when she'd crewed on a *Planet Peace* voyage, then ramped up last winter when she'd gone whale-watching off Piedras Blancas but unexpectedly become part of a sperm whale adventure. She was afraid she'd monopolized far too much of Dr. Payne's attention during the evening, both by telling her own stories and by listening attentively to his. But he seemed delighted to have an avid listener, and she considered it a spectacular opportunity to have met a leader in cetacean studies.

As the evening concluded, she joined other guests walking towards a valet area. She waited for her car, nodding as strangers congratulated her, and gazing out over distant rolling hills illuminated by a bright half-moon. *It would have been nice to share the evening with someone. Zack probably goes to black-tie events all the time. I know Meredith does. Still, I did enjoy myself.*

The drive back to her hotel was short, and she drifted to sleep between crisp sheets, images of the evening replaying themselves, but with animals, instead of humans, dressed in tuxedos and gowns.

Miranda took another sip of her tea and stroked Shadow, who began to purr. "You look so cozy, kitty. Maybe I'll take a nap, too."

"Meh," Shadow replied without opening her eyes.

I slept later than usual this morning. Still the six-hour drive was tiring.

Before tackling her unpacking, laundry, and dinner preparations, she allowed herself a few more minutes to reflect on her eventful trip.

Last night the Gala Chair had made kind remarks about her painting *Lia the Cheetah*, all the while standing in front of a huge screen vivid with a giant projected version of her work. As Miranda herself regarded the familiar image, that moment of eye contact with the beautiful animal had reminded her that she'd soon be painting a similar moment—the one she'd experienced on the water with Cory the sea otter and her pup—when both had looked her in the eyes as if to say thank you.

How united they were, the mother and offspring. How ec-

static to be reunited after the pup's rescue. And how determined the mother was to do any and everything she could to make sure her pup was safe.

Miranda's recent episodes with her own mother—the unexpected gifts, the thoughtful awareness of Miranda's taste and style, the understated sense both of pride and of protection—were new revelations that shone like sunlight sparkling on the ocean she could just see through the trees.

The sense of connection vibrated through her, making her want to rush to nearby Touchstone Beach where the local raft of otters lived in the kelp. Irrationally, she imagined talking to them, telling them she understood them better now, knew why they worked so hard to groom their pelts, feed their young, watch for predators. She knew that among those who regarded the pups as prey were not only sharks and orcas, but even adult male otters who'd been known to hold a pup for ransom, forcing the mothers to give over food.

They seem so carefree, bobbing offshore. But that's deceptive. Miranda wanted to share their special secret, promise to do her best to protect them and their young, then reach out and shake hands to seal the bargain.

Smiling at the image, she carefully extricated herself out from under Shadow, walked into her studio, and began sketching the image she would soon be painting.

40

Will Marks got an early start on Monday morning, feeling more refreshed than he had in months. He and Francine had agreed their weekend was a great success, and now they had plans to get together again in two weeks, next time she had a long layover.

His good mood made him feel entitled to a treat, so he drove down to the Embarcadero and stopped by the Starfish Bakery for a hot latte and a pecan braid before heading to Clarke Shipping.

At work, he stepped into the break room, admired the view—he never tired of it—and grabbed a plate for his pastry. When he sat at his desk, he lifted the lid off the still-hot drink, took a bite of his roll, and opened the copy of one of the local papers he'd brought from home.

His voracious appetite for news was part work, part pleasure. For his job, reading the *Wall Street Journal* and the *Financial Times* was a must. But local news mattered, too, not just as a resident, but as a local representative of the company and the industry in which he worked.

He'd get to the national and international papers in a few minutes. One of his favorites was the *San Luis Obispo Telegram-Tribune* with its impressive history of having been in continuous publication since 1869. But first, he decided to read the *Milford-Haven News*, which seldom had a scoop, but almost always offered colorful pieces about its quirky, individualist residents.

What caught his eye, though, was a piece about the shooting of a sea otter in Santa Barbara. The otter'd apparently been discovered by a local wildlife official near the place—and the time—he and Francine had been kayaking. *Found the very next day. Scary as hell!*

The shooting was still under investigation. But meanwhile, a local organization called Sea Otter Rescue was asking for any information readers might have. *Do I know anything? Did I see anyone? I'll have to talk to Francine about it.*

He'd be sure to check the SLO and Santa Barbara newspapers for further coverage. But meanwhile, he also began to wonder where, exactly, Clarke Shipping stood with regard to wildlife protection. He'd heard something about a new effort to export sea otters from the Santa Barbara coastline to one of the Channel Islands. *If I remember right, it was to protect otters from possible oil spills. But what makes people think they can determine where wildlife will wander or habituate?*

He'd make sure to read up on company policies, too, in case a reporter ever wanted to know. All in all, the article made him a little less safe, and a little more aware.

41

WE OTTER PROTECT THEM, read the bold headline. Miranda smiled, settled herself at her dining table with her morning cup of English Breakfast tea, and folded her copy of the *Milford-Haven News* so as to see the article more clearly, written by local reporter Emily Wilkins.

When Emily'd heard Miranda was being honored by the San Diego Zoo, she'd asked to write a profile article about the painter. Not caring much for the limelight, Miranda had agreed only as long as the focus stayed mostly on the animals. They'd reached a compromise when she offered that Emily could write about Miranda's wildlife research adventures, including her most recent, in Santa Barbara.

The main interview had taken place before Miranda left town on her recent travels. Then the two had met for an early dinner Saturday, when Miranda had lent Emily some sketches to include in the piece, and described some of what'd happened in the waters of the Channel Islands. But the article now in front of her was news, not the feature, which was scheduled for a week later. *I should have remembered that Emily's a journalist first, and when she gets hold of a story, she goes to multiple sources.*

Monday, February 11, 1997
Santa Barbara, California

Three Central Coast residents had a close encounter of the "otter" kind, in which a sea otter pup was saved from drowning by an environmentalist, a commercial fisherman, and an artist.

Katy Sails of Sea Otter Rescue, Doug Haliwell and Drusilla MacIntosh of D&D Charters—all in Santa Barbara—and Milford-Haven artist Miranda Jones took a day-excursion aboard the *Daxwell*, departing the Santa Barbara Harbor and heading for the Channel Islands, thirty-eight miles off shore. Also aboard were a couple from Santa Maria, Mr. and Mrs. Cedric Worthington.

The tourist trip, designed to offer glimpses of Anacapa Island with its rich, spring bloom of wildflowers, as well as area sea life, had been progressing without incident until a purse fell overboard. A young sea otter pup—a member of a protected species—swam inside and was in danger of drowning until rescued by Sails, Jones, and Haliwell.

Under normal circumstances, Sails and Haliwell would find themselves on opposing sides when it comes to sea otters. The endangered animals are considered a "keystone species" in that by feeding on urchins—a large part of their diet—they keep kelp forests from being destroyed. But commercial fishermen—many of whom depend for their livelihood upon harvesting urchins for the lucrative seafood market—beg to differ, and consider the otters irritating and even dangerous pests.

Miranda sipped her tea, and reflected that the article might not be great for tourism. First, it portrayed the trip as being run by people on opposite sides of a touchy political issue. Second, it depicted sea otters as potentially dangerous. She was unprepared for the turn the article then took into a much darker subject.

> In a separate incident, a sea otter was found shot to death the previous Thursday. Though currently under investigation, some officials speculate that the otter could have been harmed by a belligerent fisherman. Discovered washed ashore near Goleta, the nursing female was apparently battered, then shot with a pellet gun.
>
> Members of a local rescue organization later found an adolescent male pup nearby, possibly related to the dead female. They have placed the pup with a surrogate otter mother—their normal procedure in cases of abandoned offspring.
>
> Several other instances of otter shootings have been reported along the Central Coast, with none of the ongoing investigations yet closed.

Miranda put her mug down so quickly, some of the tea sloshed out on to the table. "What?" she said aloud. *Thursday . . . We didn't go as far as Goleta . . . but almost. And there we were . . . totally unaware someone that aggressive and violent must have been almost exactly where Katy and I were kayaking that day!*

She thought back to their Friday trip to Anacapa, remembering that all the crew members had been at a meeting before they embarked. But on board . . . no one had said a word. *That must have been by design, so as not to upset the tourists, like me and the Worthingtons.* Glancing down at the paper again, she realized Emily had spoken to them, too.

> Though apparently no violence against sea otters was part of the tourist trip to Anacapa, at least one passenger thought it should have been.
>
> "I just couldn't imagine what those girls were doing out

there in the water," explained Mrs. Ezmeralda Worthington, when asked about the trip. "When they were in that kayak, one of those vicious otters jumped right up and tried to bite their feet. You think the girls would have sense enough to carry weapons. But no, then they started actually swimming with the creatures! It's a wonder they weren't killed." When asked how it was that her purse fell off the boat, Mrs. Worthington had no further comment.

The environmentalist aboard had a different perspective. "It was so gratifying to see that one of our previously rescued otters is now thriving in the wild," explained Katy Sails, Director of Santa Barbara's Sea Otter Rescue (SOR). "And I was able to confirm that she has now become a mother. It was clear she recognized me from her time in captivity. Sea otters, especially young ones, are tremendously clever and curious, so when the large, bright green purse fell overboard, the pup went to investigate. It pushed itself inside, then nearly drowned because it couldn't get out. When her pup's life was threatened, the otter mom became frantic. Fortunately, I had the immediate help of both Doug Haliwell and Miranda Jones. Together we were able to save the pup, and keep the mom from inadvertently injuring us. It's a remarkable story. I never imagined I'd be so grateful to a painter, and especially to an urchin diver. It's good to know we're more on the same side than we thought."

Artist Miranda Jones, who's had several previous ocean adventures doing research for her wildlife paintings, refused to take credit for the rescue. "It's always a privilege when animals in their native habitat allow us to share their space. Until this trip, I didn't understand how clever and intelligent sea otters are. They live mostly within sight of humans, are the only creatures in the ocean with articulated paws which they use like hands, and, given that they're returning from the brink of extinction, they're tremendously resilient."

Miranda hardly remembered saying all that to Emily, but, knowing the reporter's scrupulous attention to her research and interviews, knew she must have.

"I think this trip did a lot to remind me that intelligent species have so much in common," the artist observed. "There's mind in the waters. And that's not all. There's heart in the waters, too."

Cast of Characters

Joseph Calvin: mid-60s, 6'1, gray eyes, steel-gray hair, cle
lean, handsome; CEO of Santa Barbara's Calvin Oil; eligibl
dates several women including Christine Christian.

Zackery Calvin: mid-30s, 6'2, blue eyes, dark blond hair, handsome,
lean, athletic; Vice President of Calvin Oil, works with his father;
popular bachelor; dates Cynthia Radcliffe; becomes smitten with
Miranda Jones.

Ken Casmalia (AKA "Notes"): mid-30s, 5'9, black eyes, black hair
past his shoulders, lean and long-muscled, handsome, Native American; a musician whose band often played warm-up for the Doobies;
an enigmatic man who listens more than he talks. Formerly a member of the Chumash Tribal Council; recently became Ranger for the
new Channel Islands National Park.

Stacey Chernak: late 40s, 5'6, blue eyes, blond hair, kind, submis-
sive, speaks with a Swiss-German accent; married to abusive Wil-
helm Chernak; works full-time as Clarke Shipping secretary, and
works part-time for Chernak Agency.

Christine Christian: early 40s, 5'6, aqua eyes, blond, vivacious,
beautiful, intense; special investigative reporter for Satellite-News
TV station KOST-SATV; lives in Santa Maria; frequent international
traveler; dates Joseph Calvin.

Russell Clarke: early 60s, 6'3, coal black eyes, dazzling white
teeth, dusky skin, deceptively strong, by turns charming and stern,
adopted, has unknown mixed lineage; owner of Clarke Shipping;
Stacey Chernak's employer; business associate of Joseph Calvin;
commissions Jack Sawyer to build him Milford-Haven's most magnificent seaside mansion.

Dave Dax: mid-30s, 6'1, one of two founding partners in D&D Channel Charters; an outgoing, pleasant man; a runner.

Kuyama Freeland: mid-70s, 5'7, pale gray eyes, long white hair
down her back, strong and graceful, unadorned, Native American, a
Chumash Elder.

Leo Garza: 38, 5'6, dark hair and eyes, walnut-colored skin; Warden,
California Department of Fish and Game, providing the public with

..nting and fishing information, patrols huge areas by boat, plane, truck or on foot; carries a firearm.

Ramon Gutierrez: 50, 5'8, dark hair and eyes; majordomo to Zelda McIntyre; Concierge at the building in Santa Barbara. Kind, trustworthy, dependable.

Doug Haliwell: late 30s, 6', dark-orange hair in a long crew cut that tends to stand up in spikes; an athletic man, strongly built and muscular; one of two founding partners in D&D Channel Charters; a commercial diver; a student of history.

Samantha Hugo: early 50s, 5'9, cognac-brown eyes, redhead, statuesque, sharp dresser; Director of Milford-Haven's Environmental Planning Commission; Miranda's friend; Jack Sawyer's former wife; a journal writer.

Deputy Delmar Johnson: early 30s, 6'2, brown eyes, black hair, handsome, muscular, African-American; with the San Luis Obispo County Sheriff's Department, assigned to the Special Problems Unit; originally from South Central Los Angeles.

Meredith Jones: early 30s, 5'8, teal eyes, medium-length brunet hair, beautiful, shapely, athletic; San Francisco financial advisor; Miranda's sister.

Miranda Jones: late 20s, 5'9, green eyes, long brunet hair, beautiful, lean, athletic; fine artist specializing in watercolors, acrylics and murals; a staunch environmentalist whose paintings often depict endangered species; has escaped her wealthy Bay-Area family to create a new life in Milford-Haven.

Veronica "Very" Jones: late 50s, 5'6, married to Charles Jones; mother of Meredith and Miranda, elegant member of Bay Area elite society; a more devoted mother than she seems.

Drusilla MacIntosh: 25, 5'6, long-blond hair sun-bleached, fit and strong; a competent SCUBA diver and boat tender who works for Doug Haliwell at D&D Charters, and dives for urchins for local fish markets.

Francine Mackie: mid-30s, 5'5, gold-brown hair, pert and pretty, calm and steady; has a condo in Carpenteria; works as a flight attendant for Western Pacific Airlines; dates Will Marks.

Will Marks: mid-30s, 6', dark eyes and hair, athletic build; VP at Clarke Shipping; contact of Zack Calvin's at Calvin Oil.

Zelda McIntyre: early 50s, 5'1, violet eyes, wavy black hair, voluptuous, dramatic and striking; owner of private firm Artist Representations in Santa Barbara; Miranda's artist's rep; corporate art buyer; has designs on Joseph Calvin.

Mr. Milovich: mid-50s, 5'8, salt-and-pepper close-cropped hair, currently the Jones family chauffeur; speaks with an accent from his native Montenegro; behaves with decorum.

Burt Ostwald: age unknown, 6'2, dark eyes, close-cropped blond hair, quarter-sized mole on left cheek, burly; taciturn loner; freelance construction worker; temporary-hire at Sawyer Construction—work nickname behind his back "Mole Guy"; has another primary employer.

Michael Owen: mid-40s, 5'9, blue eyes, black hair, slightly rotund; owner of Lighthouse Tavern.

Randi Raines: early 30s, 5'5, black eyes, frosted hair, cute, athletic; demanding, impatient; a talk-show host in Los Angeles; dated Will Marks.

Kevin Ransom: late 20s, 6'8, hazel eyes, sandy hair, strong jaw-line, lean, muscular without effort; Foreman at Sawyer Construction; innocent, naive, kind; tuned in to animals; technologically adept; highly intuitive; has longings for Susan Winslow.

Theo Renwick: early 60s, 6'2, blue eyes, weathered skin; Special Agent with U.S. Fish and Wildlife Service, a senior law-enforcement official responsible for the Central Coast Region.

Katy Sails: 37, 5'9, red hair; Director, Sea Otter Rescue in Santa Barbara; a passionate environmentalist.

Sandra Sandowski: 28, 5'10, short cap of blond hair; an accounting whiz who just took on D&D Charters as a new client; a runner.

Sisquoc Shunay (AKA Stephen): mid-40s, 5'7, black eyes, salt-and-pepper hair; tribal lawyer for the Santa Ynez Chumash Band.

Pete Simms: mid-50s, 5'8, hazel eyes, brown-gray hair; marine biologist; Special Agent with U.S. Fish and Wildlife Service with Piedras Blancas Field Station; lead scientist on the annual sea otter survey in California.

Gladys Wilson: mid-50s, 5'9, heavyset, long-limbed, short black hair, African-American; Office Manager at Clarke Shipping; Director of Safe Haven; a former victim of domestic violence whose wisdom and compassion now help other victims.

Mr. Cedric Worthington: mid-60s, 5'8, bald and with a stocky build; the kindly, long-suffering husband of "Mrs. Lime."

Mrs. Ezmeralda Worthington (AKA "Mrs. Lime"): mid-60s, 5'6, mousy brown hair and stocky build; a woman of firm, but not necessarily well-founded, convictions, who nonetheless is always pleased to offer her advice and opinions.

Return soon to . . .
Milford-Haven!

Coming soon

Mara Purl's
Why Hearts Keep Secrets

Book Three
in the exciting Milford-Haven saga

Enjoy the following Preview
from the book . . .

Prologue

Senior Deputy Delmar Johnson had a date with a ghost.

No matter how many times he denied the absurd notion, some unmistakable presence seemed to haunt him. Nervously, he glanced at the empty chair across the table from where he sat in the restaurant. A shiver ran down his spine. *Does it matter if my date is no longer among the living?*

He shook his head as though to clear away the tendrils of an eerie dream and force his mind into its usual, methodical approach to his cases. Though broadcast journalist Christine Christian's body had never turned up, a gnawing intuition told him the missing woman would never be found alive.

He'd made special arrangements with the missing reporter's former television station to gain access to her most recent broadcast tapes. Whatever stories she'd been working on at the time might provide some clues to her disappearance. At the very least, he'd get a sense of who she was. He'd picked up the tapes himself from KOST-TV, and they had to be returned in a timely fashion. But not before he gave them a thorough viewing. *Tonight's the night.*

Technically, he shouldn't be racking up overtime on a Sunday, but when a case wouldn't let him alone, he often found the best time to work was into the wee hours, when phones didn't ring and colleagues didn't interrupt. He justified his marginal breach of protocol by reassuring himself he was up to speed on all his other cases.

About a recent reprimand, however, he couldn't let himself off the hook so easily. Under orders from his supervisor Detective Rogers, Delmar had interviewed Mr. Joseph Calvin three months earlier. Calvin had been a friend of Ms. Christian, eventually concerned about her unexplained absence. Del had conducted the interview at Calvin's estate in Santa Barbara, but then also met Calvin in Santa Maria, allowing him to enter the premises of Chris Christian's condo. This, apparently, had been deemed inappropriate. And though nothing official had been inserted in Del's personnel jacket, the verbal admonition still stung.

Perhaps to distract himself—or maybe just to give himself something pleasant to offset the sour residue of the professional slap—Del had decided to have an early dinner at the Lighthouse Tavern. He'd only heard about it since moving here, but had no firsthand experience.

There were *real* lighthouses on the Central Coast: Point Conception in Santa Barbara to the south, Point Sur near Monterey farther north; and between the two, the Piedras Blancas light just north of Milford-Haven—the closest local lighthouse, now automated and inaccessible to visitors.

He'd been curious as to why Milford-Haven had only this

pseudo-light... realistic enough to fool the eye, but without the powerful beam that would be visible from the sea. So, after a long morning run and a session at the gym down in Morro Bay, he'd gone home to shower, shave and dress in some pressed chinos and a chocolate blazer. Then, out of uniform for once, he'd driven to the Tavern to introduce himself.

As he'd pulled into the parking lot, he'd been unsure whether he'd find a tourist trap or a quaint coastal gem. As it turned out, he liked Michael Owen. The owner looked him straight in the eye when he talked, and seemed devoted to the culinary craft, sharing details of the special he was preparing for this evening's menu. Owen was also apparently a successful businessman, as his restaurant had the reputation of drawing both tourists and locals.

Sipping wine at the bar that offered a view into the kitchen, Del asked about the history of the building, wondering why what appeared to be a real lighthouse was not being used as such. According to the story Michael recounted, if Aberthol Sayer—an entrepreneur from Milford Haven, Wales in the 1880s—had succeeded with his ambitious plan, the American Milford-Haven would've had its *own* lighthouse.

Sayer had moved to California in 1875, the successful owner of a small shipping firm. Taking stock of developments on the Central Coast, he couldn't help but notice what a bustling export center the Piedras peninsula had become for the region. Convinced that Milford-Haven's smaller point of land slightly farther south posed a treacherous landing point for fishermen, Sayer had believed that by having its own light, the area could develop a profitable fishing industry. He'd thus gone to the trouble and expense of having a defunct lighthouse on the coast of Wales dismantled and transported on one of his ships across the Atlantic, then cross-country by rail from New York to California.

Certain he'd receive the appropriate commission from the U.S. Lighthouse Board, which had been established in 1852, he'd reassembled the structure at Milford-Haven. He even had his public relations slogan ready to use: "The first lighthouse to shine on two oceans." But because he failed to receive the requisite approval, he was never allowed to install a working Fresnel in the tower. He did install a lesser light . . . but nothing bright enough to "confuse navigation," as the Board had admonished.

It turned out Sayer's light *did* shine brightly enough to attract visitors from *land*. Some hundred-plus years later, another enterprising man named Michael Owen had purchased the property with its enticing structure and turned it into the Lighthouse Tavern.

Now, as he waited for his check after an excellent meal, Del took a final sip of coffee and pressed the napkin to his lips. He turned his gaze again toward the restaurant's window to marvel again at the view—a sweep of coastal scenery that would have few equals . . . all the more spectacular at close of day, with sunset painting vivid streaks across low-hanging clouds.

After paying his bill and thanking Michael again, Del stepped outside into the March evening. The sun had sunk into the water, the sky overhead just beginning to deepen to a Prussian blue. *Nice the days aren't quite as short as they were a few weeks ago.*

The signs of early spring were everywhere on the Central Coast. Rains were no longer the steady pummelings of winter, but had shifted to blustery, intermittent storms. Tiny buds dotted the deciduous trees, and just yesterday he'd seen rows of huge iceplant flowers blooming along the beach at the Cove. Now a faint trace of jasmine hung in the air like the perfume of a woman who'd passed by and disappeared. *Ironic that in this season of renewal, the life of a young woman has almost certainly been cut short.*

Del's SUV rumbled to life and he made the short drive down Highway 1 to his workplace, glancing at a darkening sky where he could just see storm clouds hanging offshore. He suspected they'd soon overtake the coast just as his own looming depression about the case seemed certain to swamp his mood.

He parked his truck and, before locking it, lifted out the box of borrowed tapes. After climbing the stairs to the front entrance and unlocking the double-glass doors he stepped into the darkened offices shared by the North Coast branch of the County Sheriff's Department and the California Department of Forestry. His footsteps rang in the quiet hallways until he stepped into the conference room and fired up the television and VCR. After loading the first cassette he squinted in the flickering illumination from the video screen, doing his best to read the button designations of the VCR remote control.

He was hoping no one from Forestry had the same idea any time tonight . . . to use the conference room. It'd been a matter of economic necessity, placing the San Luis Obispo County Sheriff's off-site offices in shared space. The new building lacked the charm of the old-California stucco municipal structures, but Del had settled in comfortably, and—thanks to his computer expertise—enjoyed being regarded as the technical hot-shot.

At the moment, he wasn't so sure he deserved the title. He squinted again at the VCR. Certain he'd finally discerned the difference between Fast Forward and Search, he pressed something, and the blue screen sprang to life with the rapidly talking figure of a blond woman standing in a playground. Horizontal lines of static stood still as the figure raced through her story and Del struggled to find the Stop button.

Rewinding the tape, he started it again by hitting Play, deciding to be more patient with the opening designations. White letters on a field of royal blue read:

KOST-TV NEWS FILE
KOST SUNDAY NEWS MAGAZINE
REPORTER: CHRIS CHRISTIAN
ARCHIVE NUMBER: 0395749:0CC889A
SUBJECT: ADOPTION [THREE-PART SERIES]
SEGMENT ONE:
"WILL THIS LOVE LAST?:
IF I ADOPT THIS BABY WILL SHE BE MINE FOREVER?"

A second or two after the writing faded, Chris Christian appeared. Del gulped air, the sight of her animated form causing his breath to come in sudden jerks. *Nice of you to show up for our date . . . even if you are a ghost.*

Del hit the Pause button. *Get a grip, man. This is a case, not a personal relationship!*

He hit Play again, willing himself to catalog the details of her appearance. *Blond hair, tan blazer, white blouse, black slacks.* Her flawless on-camera makeup seemed out of place outdoors, but her professional appearance and calm demeanor inspired confidence, and she spoke with authority.

While the camera lens pulled back to reveal a playground Chris advanced, clasping her hands, looking down, then up at the camera, all the while introducing the topic of her show.

If Del remembered his broadcast terminology, this would be what they called the Teaser.

"Adoption," said Chris in her news-voice. "It's one of the most consuming interests among Americans today." She stepped toward a swing and sat carefully in its leather strap. "Approximately three thousand five hundred children are adopted annually in the United States, with the trend rising more than 80 percent since 1990, the year November was named National Adoption Month. And the rules have changed."

Del hit the Pause button again. Ghostly light reflected onto the slatted blinds. The image of the reporter—crisp, animated, and *alive*—disturbed him. To give himself a few seconds' break he glanced at the pale gray walls offset by black trim and looked up at the unilluminated bulbs that stared back like glassy, unseeing eyes. He turned back to the TV, hit Play and watched the screen as the camera zoomed in on Chris's face.

"Adoption used to be a private and irrevocable matter. If you, as a parent, gave up your child for adoption, you knew you would never see that child again. You also knew it would be better for the child not to suffer the confusion of meeting a parent he or she had never known.

"Each state has its own laws regarding adoption and, as a general rule, records were not legally sealed but were kept strictly confidential by a 'gentlemen's agreement'—which would now be considered an antiquated euphemism.

"While in most cases it's still difficult to find missing parents—or a long-lost child—recently developed websites mean that frustrating searches now take weeks or months, rather than years, and the Internet is brimming with information concerning all aspects of adoption. No matter how valuable adoptive parents may have been in the life of a child, as a nation, we seem consumed with uncovering our biological connections.

"Tonight we take you on the first of a three-part journey into the mysteries and emotional turmoil of adoption. If you adopt a child, will it truly be yours forever?"

After a brief pause, and a flash of white letters reading INSERT COMMERCIAL A, the program resumed. "A child of five is taken one day from the only home she's ever known," said Chris's voice-over. Del watched the screen as a wailing child held her arms out, yelling, "Mommy! Daddy!" while the adoptive parents stood paralyzed, tears streaming down their faces. On the far side of a police car, the couple—apparently birthparents—stood waiting to reclaim the child they'd given up several years earlier.

Three more three-minute reports followed, interviews with both sets of parents, interviews with Child Service professionals, and a wrap-up by Chris. Pressing Rewind, Del sat in the darkened room, deeply affected by the raw emotion he'd just witnessed. *Everyone in the story had rights; but no one seemed to have achieved a happy ending.*

Del realized he was getting drawn into the story, losing track of his own goal, which was to research the reporter. *Must mean she's doing a good job*, he acknowledged. Determined to keep an objective perspective, he hit Play and began the tape again from the beginning. This time it was details he was after—not details of the story, but of the journalist and her surroundings. *That playground . . . Miller Street Elementary in Santa Maria? I can check the photo file. Makes sense—shooting the footage close to home.*

As the segment played through, he looked at the background, pausing the tape intermittently to jot down notes or to see if he recognized the face of a passerby. *But nothing seems remarkable. I need to take an inning stretch.* He ejected the tape and held it in his hands for a moment. *Who else did I see on this tape, and not recognize? Was it someone hiding in plain sight who wished you harm?*

Chapter 1

Like a blanket dropped over a child by a watchful parent, fog had descended over the Central Coast in the cool, spring night to settle over the little town of Milford-Haven.

Miranda Jones took a final look out her studio window, observing the pre-dawn with an artist's eye. *It looks something like an unfinished landscape painting*, she decided. The trees in the foreground were filled in, but the background was still white, like gessoed canvas.

Closing the front door behind her quietly, she turned the key in the lock and brushed a long strand of dark hair away from her face, feeling the early morning chill against her cheek. It was a short walk to her driveway, and the fog had left a wet film on her dark-green Mustang. After throwing her backpack and travel purse into her front seat, she lifted the oversized duffle bag that contained her camping gear into the trunk.

Settling into the worn driver's seat, she noticed it was past time to restitch the tapestry seatcovers she'd made to hide the old vinyl.

The idle thought fled her mind like a startled bird when she thought of her plane tickets. *Are they in my purse?* Snatching the travel purse off the passenger seat, she opened it, relieved to see the edges of the tickets resting along the lining. *Monday, March 3*, the first one read. *Departure: Santa Maria, 10:20 a.m.* After confirming her return flight was scheduled for Friday, she heaved a sigh of relief and replaced the tickets snugly in her bag.

After two tries, the engine caught, and Miranda started down the long hill toward Highway 1. Although she'd made a special trip only the day before to get refueled, she checked the gauge again carefully.

Last time she'd visited her parents, her father'd offered to buy her a new car. "I gave you that old rattletrap when you were twenty-one, Mandy. My God, it was fifteen years old *then*. Since you can't afford something new, I'll buy you another one." Perhaps it was her refusal to accept his offer that made the old hunk of junk so dear to her. She bit her lip and hoped the car would once again get her all the way to the Santa Maria airport.

Had Miranda been looking out the plane's small window, she'd have seen the Pacific sparkling below against the California coastline. Instead, she sat in her cramped seat and pored over her pages. As she did with every job, she'd created a special project binder filled with clippings, research notes, Internet print-outs and preliminary sketches.

She never tired of reading about birds. The more she learned, the more fascinated she became. Their bones were hollow, their frames built light for flight. Their respiratory systems ensured ample oxygen—the wings acting as pumps that literally increased the flow of oxygen in proportion to the wing exertion. And those eyes: rapid refocusing and extreme clarity from any altitude. Above it all, they soared as if for pure joy. That was what captured her heart. Why were they so gorgeously arrayed, and why did they fly and drift on invisible updrafts? Surely it was all to make the Great Spirit happy.

Returning to her notes helped her focus on the creative aspects of the work, but she was only too aware she also had to deal with the *business* of art—never her strong suit. The world of wildlife painting was as fraught as any other endeavor with its share of competition and politics. *Wildlife Art Magazine* did an annual Art Collector's Yearbook, and Zelda McIntyre had convinced her she should buy her share of space for listing. So with her own full-color, high-quality quarter-page, she was now included in the special issue with the other 240 dedicated artists—all with superb work and impressive credentials.

Every month, it seemed, the magazine reported another contest. One was the annual Arts for the Parks competition. The catalog listed the top 100 paintings—she could only guess how many were submitted. Artists could paint any subject in any of the national parks—but detail and accuracy had to be meticulous. An artist had painted a pair of bull moose in Denali one year, and had the animals correct down to the eyelashes. His piece was disqualified, however, because he'd painted the animals in too-close proximity to each other—behavior they'd never exhibit. *What a heartbreaker that must have been*, Miranda sympathized.

While her own experience hadn't been heartbreaking, it hadn't been easy. She'd gone to Yellowstone on an invitation from her friend Al Godsey. He did brilliant documentaries, and she'd asked for years to go along on a shoot. Finally getting the chance, she'd jumped at it, and they'd spent a week in Yellowstone, filming every kind of tree, including the charred remains of the devastating burn of 1988. Her own focus had been wildlife, and she'd captured some stunning close-up shots of elk, which later became the subject for her painting.

"On Guard," she'd named her painting: a bull elk on full alert. When Zelda saw it, realizing it was eligible for the Arts for the Parks contest, she'd pushed Miranda to enter the piece. It'd meant working fast—faster than she'd ever worked on an oil—to get it completed in time for the June deadline, but she'd been proud of the work and had dared to entertain hopes of at least a regional nod. She'd received nothing but compliments. That and ten dollars would get her the next copy of the Arts for the Parks catalog.

Then there was the crowning event—the Duck Stamp Competition. Artists labored for years, yearning for the coveted prize. Many were called, few chosen. She'd settle for being a finalist sometime. For now, she'd focus on her new job. It was, after all, a bird-in-hand.

Looking now out the small window of the jet, Miranda gripped the armrests as she watched the Portland airport runway come up to meet her plane. It was a hard, but safe, landing for the crowded F100 jet.

Her trips away from Milford-Haven were generally short, but critical to her work. This one to Oregon would fulfill a commission she'd won from the State. Ever since her graduation from the small, liberal arts Carver College, she'd coveted a state commission, and now, at last, it was hers.

Her subject was to be the state bird: the Western Meadowlark, with its bright yellow breast crossed by a distinctive black V. The moment she landed the job, she looked up the little beauty on the Internet—an online encyclopedia was always a good place to start—and followed up with a trip to the San Luis Obispo Library where she'd delved into one wildlife book after another, memorizing the details of the exuberant little creature. Ultimately, her painting would hang in the State Capitol building, and there was talk of reproduction on state publications. It wasn't a stamp, but she was getting closer.

While the commission didn't come with a large paycheck, the perks more than made up the deficiency. She opened the instructions she'd printed out from her last e-mail message:

```
To:  › Mjones@mhart.net
Subj: › Upcoming trip
From: › ssarkisian@or.gov


We are looking forward to your upcoming trip
to Oregon and are sure you'll enjoy visiting
your collegiate home. You will be meeting with
Ms. Claudia Myers, State Cultural Commissioner,
regarding final details of your assignment.
Directions you requested: From the airport,
proceed East on Airport Road to the 205 South,
then go West on 84 until you dead-end at the
5, which borders the Willamette. Go left, cross
the river at the Hawthorne Bridge. Go straight
```

ahead on Main Street (one way), then left on
Broadway (one way), and left again on Columbia
(also one way). We're just down the street from
the Historical Society. Ms. Myers will brief you
on the details of your assignment. Wishing you a
good journey, S. Sarkisian.

Final details of her assignment: a euphemism for the fact that Claudia would have her check, half up front, half on delivery. Miranda rather liked receiving the money directly. It felt good to have control, and she could pay her representative Zelda the commission, rather than making Zelda do all the accounting work.

Although she knew the Portland area to some degree, she was glad of the detailed directions, as it'd been a while, and in any case, as a student she hadn't been accustomed to frequenting the hallowed halls of downtown.

After her artist's rep Zelda, the first person Miranda had told about the job was her former teacher. She'd been delighted to receive a reply from Gilroy@carveroregon.edu, and thrilled to accept his invitation to stay at his home. "Good meadowlark habitat only a couple hours away," he'd written, "and extra pencils if you run out." She'd chuckled, and quickly e-mailed acceptance of his offer for the room—and the pencils.

First, however, she had to meet with the Cultural Commissioner. Finding the building easily, Miranda pulled the white rental Ford into a visitor's spot and shut off the motor. She rummaged through her oversized purse for a brush, and pulled it twice through her long, dark hair, glanced in the visor mirror, then exited the car, notebook in hand.

The cultural office was on the ground floor of the building—three stories of brick and glass overlooking the Willamette River. No secretary sat at the reception desk, and Miranda peered around uncertainly. "Uh . . . hello?"

"Hello?" a voice answered.

"Um . . . is Ms. Myers here?"

"Ms. Jones?"

"Yes!"

Footsteps resounded on wood flooring. "Claudia Myers, Ms. Jones. Sorry we no longer have a secretary. Budget cuts."

"Oh." Apparently S. Sarkisian had moved on to greener climes, if anyplace greener than Oregon could be found. "That's all right. Please call me Miranda."

An hour later, Miranda was shaking hands in farewell, her impression of state culture having both improved and worsened. On the one hand, Ms. Myers was a thoroughly charming woman, a born diplomat, probably an able politician. In the broad strokes, her grasp of cultural matters was expansive, studied. The finer points were missing, however, and Miranda was left with the curious impression that so long as she got the meadowlark's coloring right, any rendition would do. Perhaps Monsieur Gilroy would know more. She hurried back to her rented Taurus to head for his nearby neck of the woods.

Despite the lengthening days of Spring, she began to lose the light as she headed east on 84. By the time her car angled north on 26, and east on 362nd Street, her only markers were the reflectors off mailbox posts.

The route had taken her from open highway to country lanes intermittently hemmed in by tall stands of trees that constricted the already-darkening sky. Tall maples, sturdy oaks, elegant pines stood shoulder-to-shoulder beyond where her eyes could penetrate. Tipping the ends of each branch were

the bright greens of new growth. So lush and dense with moisture was the place that it seemed the trees grew the moment
she looked away, toying with her, daring her to catch them in
motion, like a room full of dolls pretending not to move.

Her Ford rolled a little too quickly down the two-lane
road, and she glanced from side to side, catching sight of a
house here, a mailbox there. She cracked a window, inhaling
the dank, rich aroma of the forest, and heard cricketsong starting to rise as the light fell.

Glancing down at her directions, she held her finger at
"Right on SE Colorado Road." A road marker was coming up,
and she slowed to read it. Confirming this was the way, she
turned into yet another long, shadowed strip of blacktop,
which rolled away from her over a series of hills.

COLOPHON

The print version of this book is set in the Cambria font, released in 2004 by Microsoft, as a formal, solid font to be equally readable in print and on screens. It was designed by Jelle Bosma, Steve Matteson, and Robin Nicholas.

The name Cambria is the classical name for Wales, the Latin form of the Welsh name for Wales, *Cymru*. The etymology of *Cymru* is *combrog*, meaning "compatriot."

The California town of Cambria is named for its resemblance to the southwestern coast of Wales, where the town of Milford Haven has existed since before ancient Roman times, and is mentioned in William Shakespeare's *Cymbeline*.

The dingbat is an urchin, drawn by artist Mary Helsaple, and rendered graphically by cover designer Kevin Meyer. The urchin is a small, spiny animal in the echinoid class. Nearly 1,000 species of echinoids inhabit all oceans. Sea otters and other predators hunt and feed on sea urchins and their roe is a delicacy in many cuisines. The shell or "test" of sea urchins is round and spiny, found in several colors including black and dull shades of green, olive, brown, purple, blue, and red. Once the test is emptied, cleaned and dried, collectors often trim the spines, leaving a beautiful spherical, decorated shell.

LIGHTHOUSE

Each of the Milford-Haven Novels features a real lighthouse. The Anacapa Island Lighthouse is located in the Channel Islands off the coast of Southern California, on Anacapa, which is actually three volcanic islands—linked together by reefs. Positioned at the eastern entrance to the Santa Barbara Channel, the original 1912 tower held an unmanned acetylene lens lantern. In 1932, the current permanent light station was built on the island, and was the last major light station to be built on the west coast.

The 39-foot tower and fog signal were built on the highest point of the island. In 1938, under the direction of Franklin D. Roosevelt, Santa Barbara and Anacapa Islands became Channel Islands National Monument. The United States Coast Guard automated the station in 1966. In 1980, Congress designated five of the eight Channel Islands, Anacapa, Santa Cruz, Santa Rosa, San Miguel, and Santa Barbara Islands, and 125,000 acres of submerged lands as Channel Islands National Park.

The Anacapa Island Light sits atop what is known as the East Island, and the island has had various names as designated by a succession of "discoverers": in 1542, by Juan Rodríguez Cabrillo, who named the islands Las Islas de San Lucas; in 1769 by De Portola who called the islands Las Mesitas or the Little Tables; and in 1793 Captain George Vancouver renamed them Anacapa from the Chumash (sometimes called Canalino) Indian name of Anypakh, meaning "mirage," perhaps because the island frequently disappears in dense fog.

According to archeological remains and anthropological studies, the history of the Chumash people's visits to Anacapa goes back more than 5,000 years. The lighthouse is still an active aid to navigation.

Mara Purl, author of the best-selling and critically acclaimed *Milford-Haven Novels*, pioneered small-town fiction for women.

Mara's beloved fictitious town has been delighting audiences since 1992, when it first appeared as *Milford-Haven, U.S.A.©*—the first American radio drama ever licensed and broadcast by the BBC. The show reached an audience of 4.5 million listeners in the U.K. In the U.S., it was the 1994 Finalist for the New York Festivals World's Best Radio Programs.

To date, her books have won thirty finalist and gold literary awards, including the Benjamin Franklin, Indie Excellence, USA Book News Best Books, and ForeWord Books of the Year.

Mara's other writing credits include plays, screenplays, scripts for *Guiding Light*, cover stories for *Rolling Stone*, staff writing with the *Financial Times (of London)*, and the Associated Press. She is the co-author (with Erin Gray) of *Act Right: A Manual for the On-Camera Actor.*

As an actress, Mara was "Darla Cook" on *Days of Our Lives*. For the one-woman show *Mary Shelley: In Her Own Words*—which Mara performs and co-wrote (with Sydney Swire)—she earned a Peak Award. She has co-starred in multiple productions of *Sea Marks* by Gardner McKay, and plays the title role in *Becoming Julia Morgan* by Belinda Taylor. She was named one of twelve Women of the Year by the Los Angeles County Commission for Women.

Mara is married to Dr. Larry Norfleet and lives in Los Angeles, and in Colorado Springs.

Visit her website at www.MaraPurl.com where you can subscribe to her newsletter and link to her social media sites.
http://www.MaraPurl.WordPress.com.
She welcomes e-mail from readers at MaraPurl@MaraPurl.com.

CPSIA information can be obtained
at www.ICGtesting.com
Printed in the USA
FSHW01n2215080618
48927FS